Scarlet Moon

K.C. Hughes

PublishAmerica
Baltimore

First printing

ISBN: 1-4137-0073-X
PUBLISHED BY PUBLISHAMERICA, LLLP
www.publishamerica.com
Baltimore

Printed in the United States of America

To my father,

Charles E. Hughes

for your belief in me and your constant push for me to reach for the moon

Acknowledgements

I'd like to thank the guys at DeKalb County Fire Department for keeping me straight on the facts of department. I still think about that beef stew. I send many thanks to my friends at BBS who had to listen to my daily ranting about the novel. Thanks to all of you for your support, you know who you are.

I'd like to thank Patrick Williams for the cover art and Tim Schnack for the finishing touches. And of course, my editor, Sarah Cypher, at The Three Penny Editor – you are great!

And last, but not least, I'd like to thank my husband, Bobby Johnston, for having the patience of Job. You believed in me and I love you dearly.

1

I had a problem with women, not all of them, just the ones that crossed my path. I loved their sensuality, eroticism and ever so soft skin. Women smelled good, even the scent of their hair excited me. I needed to be around them, regardless of appearance. But my wife disagreed. I thought she'd be like the rest of the older generation wives who waited patiently for their husbands to stop having affairs. But Shana didn't.

I sat in the judge's reception area gazing down at the thick burgundy carpet – adding warmth, but it didn't get my mind off my failed marriage.

The judge's secretary broke my chain of thought. "Rick Edison."

She held the door to the inner sanctum. Standing tall, wearing three-inch heels put her right at six feet, just two inches shorter than me.

I walked past her and in that brief moment I heard her heart speak to me saying, *Hey sexy*. Women spoke to me all the time and all different ways. It's a sixth sense I had. I bit my tongue as I entered Judge Allgood's chamber.

The office was a direct contrast to the rich color and ardor of the reception area by the dull utilitarian furnishings. Shana sat in one of the matching leather-bound chairs, looking good for a woman divorcing her husband. She sat there like it was a financial planning meeting instead of a divorce. As for me, it was hard to hold on to the bad feelings; I got what I deserved.

But still.

When I moved to sit down, the judge stopped me. He sat behind the desk, the folds of his robe looked as if it swallowed him. He reminded me of one those old 'milk does a body good' commercials where the little boy, dressed in a grown man's suit, drinks milk and is transformed into a full grown man by the next scene.

"No need to sit," he said in a surprisingly powerful voice. "We are downhill from here." I wondered how such a little man could have such a voice like that. When he stood up, he seemed even shorter.

A second thought made me slouch down to minimize my imposing height to his. Maybe he would cut me some slack and give me more visitations with my daughter.

Who was I fooling? Why was it that all of a sudden I cared to be a good father to my baby girl? When we were a family, all I did on weekends was nurse hangovers. I can't count the times I melded with the couch instead of watching Dana turn cartwheels in the backyard. But booze helped the guilt subside while sleeping with the others, and I always suffered the consequences the next day.

"Mr. and Mrs. Edison, please stand and raise your right hand."

The seriousness of the situation suddenly hit me. My wife was actually divorcing me. I looked around for the judge's secretary, more out of panic than lust, and could have kicked myself when I saw Shana giving me the eye. I kept hearing the words of my old school buddy, New York, reverberating in my head, "You brought this shit on yourself." They called him New York because he always had something to say about everything, even though he'd never been to New York.

"Do you hereby swear that the petition for divorce in Fulton County Superior Court of Georgia is true and correct to your knowledge?"

"I do," we said.

Shana kept her eye on the judge, standing there, swirling the tennis bracelet I bought her a couple of years ago.

"And do you also swear that neither is under any undue influence to sign the divorce papers?"

"I do."

"Then, given my authority under Georgia State Statute, I hereby dissolve the union of Shana and Rick Edison. Shana, you may take back your maiden name."

That was it. I was a single man. Somehow it didn't feel all that great. After Trina, the judge's secretary, had me sign the final paperwork, I attempted to catch up with Shana. I didn't know what to say, exactly, but I thought I could make a good start with "I'm sorry."

When I walked out of the court building, I looked for her car in the parking lot. I didn't see her vehicle so I tried her on her cell phone. I wanted to scream into the phone after the fifth unanswered ring, because I knew she was avoiding me.

I left the Fulton County Superior Court and passed all the sprawling growth in Midtown Atlanta. Condos, lofts and hi-rise rentals crammed the streets of what was once a desolate playground for seedy inhabitants. I remember getting excited when I saw all the growth, thinking more women moving to town. But today, whether it's new or old, sex just didn't faze me. No matter how I tried to fend it off, I was pissed off that Shana divorced me.

I took Memorial Drive, headed toward my two-bedroom apartment in

Stone Mountain when some idiot in a green Camry jumped in front of me. From my rearview mirror, I could see the white smoke coming from my screeching tires as I pounded the breaks. I rolled down my window and gave the driver the finger. When he had the balls to shoot me one back, I accelerated the Expedition past him and immediately jumped in his lane and pressed my brakes, causing his tires to smoke. I kept my vehicle a safe distance in front of him until he turned off.

I found one of those Post apartment communities that boasted luxury living. The only luxury quality was the luxurious price tag. I signed a year's lease for nine hundred sixty bucks a month and I wouldn't have been able to make the rent and child support had it not been for my schedule at work. Since fire fighters work twenty-four-hour shifts, by the fair labor laws, we get two days off for every shift worked. This flexible schedule afforded me the opportunity to work odd security jobs at grocery stores during my forty-eight-hour hiatus. In fact, the security jobs played a major role in my divorce. Women loved a man in uniform.

As I entered my apartment, that feeling of loneliness engulfed me. I looked around the barren walls. There were no silk flower arrangements on the coffee table, no pictures on the walls or any sign that a woman lived there. Even though I had been there nearly two months, today felt different. I should have asked Judge Pee Wee whatever happened to, *What God bought together, let no man take asunder.*

Fuck it! I decided to wound my pride and call her. I hesitated after I yanked the cordless from the charger, but I went through with it and punched the ten digits to what was once my home. The phone rang until I heard her voice on the answering machine.

I swallowed and spoke into the phone, "Hey baby," I said hoping she'd pick up. "If you are there, please pick up." Shana never wanted to go with voice mail service because she said the five bucks monthly charge would pay for a decent machine in just one year. She was right. "Well, I just wanted to call to tell you that I was thinking about you and wanted to know if you want to get together for lunch or something. Call me when you get this. Bye baby."

After waiting for her to call me back, I dozed off and didn't wake up until the next morning. The sun emerged through the horizon as the birds chirped their morning melody. This time of the day used to give me a sense of renewal, but now I wished I could have slept through it.

Having explained my marital situation to my Battalion Chief, he politely demanded that I take the week off. With nothing to do, I thought to check the voice mail to see if maybe Shana called while I slept. All I heard was that familiar smug voice saying, 'You have no new messages.'

I muddled through the morning, keeping a watch on the clock for a decent time to start drinking. I wanted to forget about the rejection, but I had a motto never to drink before the sun went down. But since it was May in Atlanta, that didn't happen until eight in the evening. So I made adjustments to my motto and went to Dugan's on Memorial Drive for a cold one.

Dugan's octagon-shaped bar smelled of spilled liquor on old carpet. The place catered to no one that particular morning and somehow that was inviting. I sat down at the bar and ordered an Icehouse. It went down cold and welcoming.

After the lunch crowd from the area's dealerships and industrial parks came and went, I had a mind to go home, but I decided to call Shana. After she refused to answer my call, I made another call.

The happy hour crowd sauntered in with their talk of the day's corporate banter, and I drank with them. The atmosphere offered more vim and vigor and I drank more beers. Then she came and the next thing I knew I was in Trina's bed making vindictive love to her, a complete stranger. Then my cell phone rang. Not thinking, I jumped off her and quickly answered it.

"Hello," I said, holding my breath.

Before I heard a word from the other end, the long-legged secretary spoke, "Come back to bed and finish what you started."

"Same old Rick, I see." And Shana hung up.

I left immediately. I tried calling her back, but she never answered, so I went home to a bottle of tequila and four walls.

When I dragged myself off the couch the next morning, I vowed never to drink again because I had a headache the size of Rhode Island. I spent most of the day nursing my hangover with intermittent bouts of sleeping and eating. In between naps, I called Shana and spoke to her machine again. I really needed to tell her that the woman from last night meant nothing to me. After the third message, I was pissed off and went to the pantry for some Cheetos. When I reached in, I saw a bottle of Jose Cuervo that I had forgotten about. So much for my vows.

After an all-day drinking binge, my liquid courage doubled that of my actual courage. I decided to call Shana and give that bitch a piece of my mind. I found the cordless and had to remember my old number. I spoke to the machine, again.

"This is your husband and I demand to talk to you. You can't keep putting–"

"Rick, why are you calling me?" Shana picked up. "What do you want?"

"I want to talk about last night." I sat up, more attentive. "Turn the answering machine off so we can talk."

"Talk? Now you want to talk? What about when I tried to talk to you about the other women? What about that woman last night...." she hesitated and I could just see her holding the phone and staring at the ceiling, disgusted. "You know what, you don't have to explain anything. We are divorced and you can do whatever you want to whomever you want. Anyway, I have to go, I have an emergency at the hospital with one of my patients."

"Fuck your patient. I made you what you are and I can take it away–"

"Good-bye, Rick, forever," she said and simply hung up.

I stared at the phone and out of rage threw it across the room, breaking the only lamp I owned. I stood alone and in the dark, uncertain of my self-worth. I found my way to the couch and passed out.

I was yanked from a bottomless sleep by the pounding sound at the door. For an instant I did not know where I was. Looking around, I found the comfort of my own apartment. Sluggishly, I got off the sofa and tried to flatiron the wrinkles in my clothes with my hands. That did not work. I looked through the peephole and saw two white men dressed in what looked like polyester suits. One wore government-issued gray and the other wore a brown polyester blend.

I opened the door and squinted at the assault of the sunlight.

Gray suit backed up ever so slightly as he reached for his badge and offered it. "I'm Detective Leicky with Atlanta Homicide and this is Detective Biddings," he said as he nodded toward brown suit.

"Are you Rick Edison?" Biddings asked. He was shorter than Leicky, with a full head of salt and pepper hair, though I thought he might be wearing a toupee.

"Yeah that's me."

They looked at each other. "May we come in?" Leicky asked and motioned forward, not waiting for a nod or any kind of welcome.

I looked at both detectives and thought no harm in letting them in. Probably a burglary occurred in the complex that they were investigating. They walked into the living room. No foyer – that would have cost an additional fifty-five dollars a month. I noticed the one named Leicky had a pear-shaped torso, rounded near the waist and skinny legs that were disproportionate to his upper body mass. His eyebrows protruded menacingly, taking over the other features of his otherwise nondescript face.

"Let me throw some water on my face. I'll be right back."

Leicky jumped in without a beat. "Why don't we talk first? Where were you last night between the hours of eleven and two this morning?"

I looked around wildly. I don't know much, but I do know that when a detective asks your whereabouts between a time frame, it's not a good sign.

"I was here with Jose."

"Jose who?" Biddings asked.

I raised my eyebrows and simply said, "Cuervo."

Biddings looked down as if he were checking for dung on his shoes. His slim build went well with the tan he had and the more I thought of his vanity, the more I believed he wore a rug.

"I understand you were just recently divorced," Leicky asked.

"Yes, and?"

Biddings and Leicky looked at each other again and I began to worry.

"Detectives, what is going on?" My adrenaline pumped harder and faster. I looked from one to the other. They seemed to be disappointed.

"Mr. Edison, your ex-wife has been murdered. We need you to identify the body."

2

We met in 1982 on a bus trip to Washington DC for a black spring break picnic. Because of the R&B chart topping single, *Le Freak*, someone coined the spring break fling as 'Freak-Nik' and to this day, the name remained the same with only the venue changing, moving from DC to Atlanta to Daytona Beach.

I saw Shana on the bus but I was too busy acting up with my boys talking about all the DC honeys we were going to bang. It wasn't until we were at a dance at the Armory that I really saw her. When the DJ played the long version of *Jam on Revenge*, the 'wikki-wikki' song, Shana tore up the dance floor with her graceful hips. On the somber bus ride home, I found out that she had brains, too.

She went to Morris Brown College majoring in psychology and I went to Atlanta Metropolitan College, where I studied HVAC instead of business administration – no stiff shirt and tie for the rest of my life. I dropped out after two semesters when I got hired on at the fire department. Shana stayed in school and finished her Bachelor's degree before going on to graduate school at Atlanta University for another four years. She got her Master's and went for her Ph.D. She would've completed her doctorate on time had she not gotten pregnant and had our baby girl.

That served as a turning point in my life. I had a decent job with the Fulton County Fire Department and Shana was headed for glory as a psychologist. One day when I was in the kitchen cooking, lending a helping hand, I saw her breast-feed Dana. That moment proved how quickly a man could evolve from the excitement of seeing breasts as sexual objects to realizing that they were purposeful parts for nurturing an infant. I stood in the archway to the den, crossing the threshold to adulthood. I walked over, kneeled on the carpet and asked her to marry me.

The ride to the city morgue was worse than being in the judge's chamber. After the nefarious words, *We need you to identify the body,* I don't remember how I got dressed or how I made it down the flight of stairs to the unmarked police car, but what I did remember was the sinking feeling of falling into quicksand. The bitter morass of self-pity and pain yanked at my heart.

We drove in silence for the entire trip. I gazed out of the window and connected to nothing on the outside. Not the sprawling growth, the women, nor the scorching heat. All that mattered was that my wife was murdered.

My head was spinning as Detective Biddings turned into the morgue, located next to the East Precinct on Ponce de Leon. As the car went over the second speed bump in the parking garage, my stomach churned and I reached for the door handle. Since this was the back of a police car, there were no handles. Too late. The tequila coupled with the detective's driving came up on the floorboard.

"Oh shit," Leicky hollered in disgust.

After the cleanup, I steadied myself for the walk to the building. We walked through the parking deck to the entrance. The gray slab structure was just that: gray concrete gloom. The architecture for government buildings fell short of aesthetic beauty. The small windows offered employees the same inadequate viewing area as the DeKalb County Jail. No wonder government workers always seemed to be in a terminally bad mood; they were jailed at nine and paroled at five.

The two detectives took me through the main door and Leicky pushed a buzzer on the wall intercom system. There was a second buzzing sound, the bolt clacked free and Leicky pushed the door open and led us up to the security desk in the main lobby. Now, I know that I'm not the sharpest knife in the wood block, but I didn't understand why such security measures were needed for a *morgue*.

We walked down a hallway that had plain, tiled floors and cinder block walls. When we came to the only door in that corridor, Leicky opened it to reveal steps. We took the stairwell to the basement. Maybe they made a terrible mistake. All I had to do was to confirm that the body wasn't Shana's and I'd be on my way.

As we descended, I noticed the smell. It got stronger the further down we got. At first it smelled like a bathroom choked up with Lysol. Then another smell attacked my nostrils. It smelled like raw ground beef that had been left out overnight. As we exited the stairwell and entered the basement, the smell became so offensive that I thought I would puke again.

I was no stranger to bad smells. Working as a fireman, I knew the smell of burning flesh. I recalled the first time I smelled it. I was nine months on the force when the call came in on a burning house on Stewart Avenue. When our unit arrived, all we could do was control the blaze. After the fire abated, we went in for routine investigations, looking for signs of arson and so forth, but what we found was a smoldering body in the kitchen. The smell was so acrid, it reminded me of spoiled pork cooking on a char-grill. Joe, my mentor, pointed out the cause of the fire. Mr. Sizzle had a small Pyrex glass with open-ended holes for smoking crack. The final report on the fire came some weeks after, and stated that he used the stove to light his crack pipe, and accidentally burned his hair and everything on the lot.

We made it to the observatory. It was a small room with a glass partition between the meat locker and us. Leicky gave me a talk before he gave the go-ahead.

"Mr. Edison, when he brings the body, I want you to take deep, steady breaths."

I nodded.

The assistant medical examiner opened a stainless steel draw and slid out a long metal tray that held a body covered in a midnight blue tarpaulin.

My resolve was back. I knew it was a mistake. I just had to go through the motions of confirming that is was not Shana. I braced myself. Seeing a dead body was something that I had not let myself get used to.

The slim, Asian American assistant transferred the body from the stationary tray to a gurney and wheeled it next to the glass partition. He hesitated, leaned over and spoke into the embedded microphone next to the glass. "Are you ready?"

How can anybody ever be ready? I wanted to ask, but didn't.

At certain times in life, time stands still. This was my time. I cannot remember whether it was the fact that I stopped breathing or the fact that the ME went meticulously slow when he unzipped the body bag. When he parted the flaps and looked up, my gaze fell to the sight that lay on the other side of the partition.

It was Shana. A flush of remorse came over me as I realized how much I hurt her. I recalled the endless late-night conversations of her pleading with me to stop sleeping with every woman that crossed my path. Instead of listening to her and working out my infidelity issues, I kept on doing the same thing over, expecting different results.

Had I not been an asshole, I might've been able to save her from such brutality. Reality set in that she was dead and a large hole grew in my soul. But something was terribly wrong. After I bumped my head on the glass trying to get a closer look, I saw it. Her eyes had been gouged out with some kind of pointed object. In my rage at the assault of my wife, I pounded on the glass with my fists so hard it shattered in large pieces. The assistant moved Shana's body away from the flying shrapnel, and that was the last time I saw my wife.

3

When Leicky and Biddings escorted me out, they took me to an office without windows. Another coroner clad in surgical blues sat behind a cluttered desk. Her sharp-eyed gaze noticed my wounded wrist. Immediately she came to my aid.

"What happened?" She took my hand and examined it.

When I failed to speak she looked at the detectives and Leicky nodded toward the lab where Shana's body was stored.

"I'm Dr. Van Hart."

Even if my wife had not been murdered, I would not have remembered her name. I sat there letting that petite package of a woman examine my hand. The cut needed stitches. She began the sutures while Leicky stood by the doorway looking on. He paid more attention to the doctor than the actual wound and she didn't seem to notice. For a moment, it looked as if he was going to start flirting with her.

As I slumped in the chair, stupefied, I kept seeing the frozen image in my mind of my wife lying dead on a cold table with her eyes bludgeoned out. At that second, I got a moment of clarity to ask about her abominable fate.

"How did she die?" I swallowed hard.

She looked at the detectives. They remained standing as I sat getting my wrist stitched. Leicky nodded his approval to tell me.

"First of all the autopsy report indicated high levels of an opiate called Oxycotin. I don't know if you are familiar with it."

"No, never heard of it."

"It's the brand name for a prescription drug oxycodone hydrochloride," she explained as I felt the first prick of the suture needle. "Oxycontin is derived from the same opium plant as heroin and is highly addictive." She paused and looked up at me. "Was your wife suffering any type of chronic pain?"

"Not at all. She is...." I stopped, pursed my lips and watched as the thread weaved out of my flesh. "She was a psychologist and sometimes referred patients to doctors that could prescribe medication."

The doctor stopped patching my wrist, got up and walked around to her desk. She found the file she was looking for and wrote a note.

"What is it?" I saw Leicky jotting down a note in his notepad. I looked at him suspsiciously.

"Mr. Edison, this is a murder investigation and I see Ms. Edison as someone who had access to drugs and used them recreationally," Leicky said, emphasizing the 'Ms.'

I stared at him in disbelief and without realizing it, I jumped up, grabbed him by his polyester jacket and slugged him with my cut hand.

Biddings grabbed Leicky before he could return the punch. The doctor moved in quickly from behind the desk and planted herself in between us. She managed to control the flare up and I began feeling the pain of my cut wrist.

"If you assault me again," Leicky said. "I'll write you up for every infraction of the law on the books." He swiped a hand across his hair in a vain attempt to straighten it out.

"Then don't refer to my wife as a pill-pushing dope fiend." In my rage, a squirt of spittle left my mouth and landed on the medical examiner.

"Let's not jump to any conclusions until we analyze all the evidence, Detective Leicky," she said as she wiped the saliva off with her jacket sleeve. All of a sudden, she was tougher than I thought, with effectiveness of someone twice her size. She had dark auburn hair with skin the color of coffee. Her makeup-free face only made me look into her perfectly spaced almond shaped eyes. She exuded some kind of motherly warmth that made me want to please her. I sat back down.

Leicky calmed down too, swiping his hand across his hair, again.

The doctor found the needle and resumed my stitches. I wanted to ask her when was the last time she operated on a living person but I quickly nixed that thought.

"Please tell me how my wife died," I said.

"Mr. Edison, I'm afraid it's not going to be good news. Why don't you let the detectives do their jobs and investigate your wife's murder?"

I hesitated and grabbed the metal paperweight off her desk and fondled it.

"Dr. Vanguard, I have–"

"Van Hart," she interrupted. "Dr. Van Hart."

Out of my peripheral vision, I saw Leicky lower his head to conceal his smirk. If the good old doctor hadn't been piercing the needle in my skin at that very moment, I swear I would've slugged him again. "I have a right to know how she died."

She stopped as she pulled the stitch through and looked at me. "It's never easy, but in this case I'd say it might be a bad idea to say too much now, for you sake–"

"Freedom of Information Act," I said.

She shrugged her shoulders. "Have it your way." She reached over and grabbed the same file she that she jotted down that note after I told her Shana was a psychologist. I noticed reluctance on her part.

"After finding high levels of Oxycontin, we ran more tests and frankly, your wife died of heart failure."

"That's it?" I said in disbelief. "Millions of people die of that. Why was that so hard–" Something made me stop. Then it came to me. Dr. Van Hart lowered her head seemingly anticipating my next question.

"Why were her eyes gouged out?"

I previously thought Leicky and Biddings knew the fate of my wife, but the way they leaned in when I asked the question led me to believe they were about to find out the same time as me.

"Again, I wish you'd reconsider and let the police department handle it."

"Tell me."

She sighed. "Test results show dried powder residue in the crevices of the sphincter muscles as well as severe abrasions."

I was confused. "What does that mean?"

She looked at the two detectives standing against the wall. "It means that your wife was sodomized."

I didn't know the medical term for that feeling you get when your heart drops to your gut, but the blood drained from my head and I had to grab the chair handles to keep myself in the horizontal position.

"Some rubber manufacturers lubricate their product with a petroleum-based substance and others use a talcum-based lubricant. I sent samples to the lab in Phoenix to get all manufactures that use talcum-based lubricant."

But that still didn't explain the dreadful picture in my mind of Shana's eyes. "What about her eyes?"

"I'm getting to that." She paused for what seemed like an hour. The room was so quiet that I could hear the second hand of her wall clock ticking. When she spoke, she failed to make eye contact with me. "Her eyes were gouged out while she was still alive so she wouldn't be able to see him while he sodomized her."

If the detectives thought I had anything to do with it, I was pretty sure they dismissed their assumptions.

Dr. Van Hart looked up at the detectives in time to see Leicky turn his head toward the wall to hide the rage. Biddings broke the silence.

"Mr. Edison, let me take you home." He gently tugged on my forearm.

I quickly yanked it from his grip. "Go home? Go home to what? My wife has been raped and brutally.... I don't think that's a strong enough word for it. More like barbaric. And you want me to just go home?"

"Let us do our jobs," Leicky joined in. "The doc is sending out for more lab tests. And once we get the test back from the rape kit, and the crime scene dusted for prints, we'll have a complete snapshot of what we're looking for,"

If he was sore at the punch I gave him, it wasn't evident.

"Before I leave I just want to understand one thing." I looked straight at Dr. Van Hart. "You said earlier that she died of heart failure. I don't understand the connection."

Dr. Van Hart dropped her gaze and looked down. "When the body experiences so much trauma, the heart simply stops beating. It's the body's ultimate self-defense mechanism."

I lay in the backseat of the detective's car curled in a fetal position. I don't know how we got through the traffic to my apartment. I stared vacantly at the floorboard of the vehicle, hoping it was some kind of bad dream and that I'd wake up with Shana still breathing. But the vision of her mutilated body on the cold table replayed in my mind like a videotape on repeat mode. For the first time in my life, I thought of suicide. Then I thought of Jerome.

About six months ago, a blaze occurred at one of the renovated breweries on Northside Drive, the trendy section of Atlanta. Following the death of her mother, a young lady got a huge insurance check that paid for the simple loft. One evening after partying too much, she fell asleep with candles burning. The smoke inhalation killed her in her sleep, but her four-year-old daughter remained trapped behind weakened rafters, screaming for her mother. That's where Jerome found her. He was physically able to rescue her, but he knew as well as we did that he couldn't cross the threshold to the room where the little girl coughed in gut-wrenching spasms. Instead, he said everything was going to be all right. Word had it he told her to lie down, close her eyes and he promised she'd be with her mother when she woke up. The little girl died a few yards from him. Jerome never recovered from that night. A month later, he hung himself from his second-story deck.

Suddenly I realized I had something to live for. Dana needed me now more than ever. How do you tell a bright little girl that her momma was dead? It crossed my mind to ask Leicky but I decided not to. What do white people know about pain anyway?

When I finally made it to the apartment I forced myself into the shower, then I set out to Douglasville to get my daughter. On the way, I called my sister to tell her that I'd be there in an hour.

Driving west on I-20 in the afternoon was dubbed the sunshine slowdown. I drove right into the sun and did not bother turning on WJZF 107.5 to tune into the smooth jazz. I just drove. My eyes burned from a combination of sun and a mild hangover from last night's tequila. I had to keep blinking, to stave off the gargantuan headache that was on its way in. Traffic stayed light in the afternoon and I drove faster than normal get to Dana's school before the 2:45 dismissal.

Chapel Hill was one of the newer schools in Douglasville. With Atlanta's growth, there had been as many new schools built as office towers. I remembered a couple of years back I had to call the school. I made a big stink because the secretary told me there was no one by the name of Dana Edison enrolled at Chapel Hill Elementary. I called her an illiterate government worker and asked how she managed to pass the pre-employment test that was required of all government employees. Her next words made me feel as small as a mite. She simply asked if I wanted Chapel Hill Elementary in DeKalb County or Douglas County. When I profusely apologized, she mentioned that it happened all the time. Atlanta has so many schools they had to recycle names.

While the receptionist sent for Dana, the principal, Mrs. Jenkins, came around to speak to me. Why couldn't she be in a staff meeting or something? She stood five foot six, took care of her shape and wore the crispest Ann Taylor suit I'd ever seen. I remember getting aroused when I met her last year. She reminded me of Shana, an African-American professional aligning with self-sufficiency and independence. I gravitated towards her and by the weekend, we were sleeping together. After she began sending notes home with Dana, I put an end to our affair.

When I explained to her the reason for Dana's early release, I saw the twinkle in her eye. What a sick bitch, I thought but didn't say. When I politely declined her invitations to help with meals and errands, Dana walked in and saved her from further groveling.

As soon as Dana got in the car she started in with the questions.

"Daddy, we fixin' to go?" Dana said.

"Baby, what did Daddy tell you about talking country?"

"You're right. I'm sorry. Daddy, where are we fixin' to go?"

I did not have the energy to correct her. I just looked at her pretty face and pulled out of the school's parking lot. When I passed the school zone and was able to speed up I decided to wait to break the news that her mother had gone to heaven.

"Sweetie, how would you like to stay at Aunt Aisha's house for a few more days?"

"Yeah." Her elation rose and then it dropped. "I don't know, because Julius, the kid next door, keeps pulling my hair."

Kids' frame of reference was so small. Had she known that Julius liked her and just didn't know what to do to show affection, she would have understood the hair pulling.

As usual, Aisha had a cup of coffee in one hand and a cigarette in the other. She looked at Dana, then up at me suspiciously. She must have seen something of the truth there, because she looked back at Dana, worried now.

"Dana, I think Mrs. Johnson is picking the okra from her garden today. Why don't you see if she'd let you help."

"You mean I don't have to do my homework first?"

"This time we'll let it slide. Just change your clothes and go help Mrs. Johnson."

Such patience with kids even with two of her own, Christopher and Chloe. Aisha was my older sister who swore she had first rights to that name. She even wrote a letter to Stevie Wonder asking for royalties from the song *Isn't She Lovely*. He never wrote her back.

Aisha was able to get on with BellSouth at the onset of their hiring frenzy. New technology coupled with the demand for more bandwidth gave her a foot in the door the of the South' s largest telecommunications company. She began as a wage scale ten and studied for the test that would land her a higher-paying job. Finally she made it to a Service Consultant, a liaison between large business customers and BellSouth's inner departments. She excelled at her job, knowing the value of web-based business utilities before its time. She did so well that they promoted her to a supervisor over a team of 16 SCs. With her team setting productivity records, she was promoted to a Specialist, working from home writing methods and procedures for service consultants throughout BellSouth's nine-state region. That was how Shana and I decided to buy our house in Douglasville.

Aisha asked if I wanted any coffee and when I declined, she poured herself another cup and sat down at the kitchen table with her ashtray. I didn't know how to tell her that Shana was murdered but I started with the early-morning knock on my door, and the rest of the story found its way out.

When I finished recounting all that I knew, Aisha lit her third cigarette with a pensive look on her face. The house seldom smelled like smoke though, just coffee. Aisha sat in contemplation, thoughtful but on the verge of tears. We sat in silence for a moment and it was Aisha who broke it.

"Why don't you let Dana stay here for the summer? School will be out in a few weeks."

I had not thought of that. How was I going to manage getting her to school from the other side of town? The more I thought about Dana staying with Aisha, the more it made sense. That would give me time to transfer Dana to a school in Stone Mountain by next schoolyear.

"Have you thought about arrangements?" Aisha asked.

"Funeral arrangements?" That was another thing, *shit*. I had no idea where to begin.

"If it's all right with you," Aisha said, "I can make all the arrangements. I'll check with you for the big decisions."

This woman was an angel. I realized how helpless I was. I have always depended on women for love and belonging and everything in between. In that moment I wanted to crawl back inside my mother's womb and forget about all the pain and suffering I was experiencing. No wonder babies cry when they first come out, they must inherently know that it's downhill from that point on.

4

Aisha arranged for a beautiful gravesite service at Memorial Gardens Eternal Rest Haven on Candler Road in Decatur. The sun shone brightly and the birds provided a hymn. The pastor, though, took it upon himself to advertise his funeral services during the interment, and repeatedly said that no one is ever turned away at his funeral home. I stayed on after the official ceremony to see my wife's casket lowered into its final resting place.

I sat on the folding chair thinking about life with Shana shortly after our marriage. Dana was growing fast and we had to sneak to make love. The thrill of the prowl turned me on to new heights of eroticism. Shana realized I had a hefty appetite for sex and she played into the pillage. But when Dana required more attention from Shana than I was willing to give up, I felt rejected and sought comfort between other women's thighs.

Two weeks passed since I buried my wife and I needed to get back to work. The stitches dissolved, leaving a long scar that looked like I tried to commit suicide by slashing my own wrist. My Battalion Chief gave permission to take a full month off with bereavement pay, but I was going stir crazy. I decided to call make arrangements to return to work early. When I reached for the phone, it rang.

"Mr. Edison, this is Effie May at the Emory Clinic," she said with trepidation. "I am terribly sorry for your loss."

I had no idea how to respond, so I simply said, "Thank you." Effie May was Shana's secretary, taking patient calls and filing insurance forms. I met her on several occasions and she reminded me of the secretary on *Ferris Bueller's Day Off,* forming the letter 'O' with her mouth when she spoke. I asked Shana why she hired an older white lady instead of giving the position to an African American professional. She simply said that she didn't want her patients to feel intimidated by the presence of a buppie snob secretary that secretly polished her silverware with her napkins for fear of catching some dreaded restaurant disease. I wish I could take back all the terrible names I called her after she told me that.

"I'm calling you about Doctor Edison's personal belongings."

So this is how companies bury the dead. They get rid of personal effects, thereby disassociating themselves with the deceased. I just buried my wife and now Emory wants me to clear out the office. So much for the grieving process. "I can come now." And I hung up.

I experienced great apprehension as I drove to the place where Shana worked. My first mind told me to hire a mover, but I decided that it was time to face the music. Plus I had nothing else to do.

When I reached the Psychiatric Clinic, I glanced at the hospital where Shana's body was found. I wanted to walk over and ask each employee had they seen anything out of the ordinary the night of the murder, but I changed my mind and parked the car instead. I raced from the heat to the front entrance.

The Psychiatric Clinic consisted of a rectangular building with as many paned windows as I could count. The only entrance was covered with a teal cloth awning that read *Clinic* across it.

I made it up to the office and was greeted by Effie May.

"Mr. Edison, I am so sorry about your loss." She clasped her hands together and stood there with her silver hair like a Catholic school nun. I was pretty sure she had attended the funeral but for the life of me, I couldn't remember.

"I didn't want to rush you, but the Clinic forced my hand."

"I should have been here sooner but…."

Then she patted me on the shoulder.

I didn't know how much she knew about the divorce; probably nothing. I understood why Shana hired her. She conveyed a warm spirit that was both inoffensive and enchanting.

She let me in Shana's office and turned to leave. "Take your time and let me know if you need anything."

When I was alone in her office, I could have sworn I smelled a whiff of Shana's favorite fragrance, White Linen. It was so familiar that I felt a strong pressure build and I wept.

I looked around and didn't know where to start. Why hadn't I thought to bring a box? I sat on the oversized chenille couch, held my head in my hand and cried. I must have been crying loud as Effie May appeared at the door with a box.

"Oh, let it out. Don't you worry." She placed her arm around me.

"Why did she have to die, why? It should have been me. I was the asshole."

"Oh, sweetie, remember that God's Will won't take us where God's grace can't keep us. She's in a better place."

"You really think she is?" I asked, wondering what made me question that statement then when in the past I thought it was just rhetorical spiritual babble.

"Oh heavens, yes," she gave me a matronly look, "just believe."

When she was satisfied that I was all right, she left the office. I collected myself and mustered the courage to walk around to Shana's desk.

The office was contemporary, with angled furnishings and stainless steel fixtures. I noticed that she didn't have a computer on her desk, and remembered her telling me that some people with mental illnesses view them as offensive. She went on about how she attempted to make the office conducive for progress. In fact, I remember how she had to strategically place the wall clock where it was out of the patients' view, explaining that the concept of time made some people anxious. I looked up and saw a small stainless steel wall clock behind the patient couch.

I took a deep breath and began looking through her things. The first thing I saw was her ball-bearing Rolodex card file. I grabbed it and quickly scanned its contents. Nothing out of the ordinary. I got up, walked over to the banker's box and sat it next to the desk. I placed the Rolodex inside.

The telephone sat next to the Rolodex, a hi-tech Cisco IP Phone, whatever that meant. It had a bunch of soft keys with a three-by-five LCD screen. The menu-driven readout gave a listing of current options and when I pressed the directory key, more options came up, one of which was received calls. Out of curiosity I pressed the soft key for that option and to my surprise, a list of calls with the number, date and time stamp as well as the name showed up on the screen. I scrolled down to the last day of Shana's life and saw that I called twice that morning, Emory Clinic called once, a host of private names and private numbers showed up, including three calls from a J. Kennard. I exited out of the screen and returned to the desk.

On the other side of the telephone, there was a 5x7 photo of Dana standing in a pool. She beamed with joy. Somehow I didn't remember that scene. I placed the picture in the box. Then there were the traditional desk accessories, pencil cup, paper clip dispenser, cardholder, a Day Minder appointment book and letter tray, all in a slate gray color. I scooped them all and placed them in the box. I reached for the box of Kleenex and sniffed, wanting and needing to smell her again. I placed it in the box.

After I cleaned off the desk, I started on the inside. I opened the lap drawer and saw a multitude of pens, pencils and rubber bands. I transferred those to the box. I saw a lonely key and decided to leave it there. Then I went to open the draw on the left-hand side and it was locked. I reached back in the lap drawer, removed the key and inserted it in the lock. It worked. I saw

Shana's laptop and lifted it to the box. On second thought, I decided to boot it up and see the contents.

While the machine booted, I searched through the remainder of the drawer. I saw an 8x10 photo of Shana and me at one of those tiki bars in Jamaica. For our first anniversary, we left Dana with Aisha and took off for week in Montego Bay. I wondered why she hadn't destroyed the photo instead of hiding it in the drawer. I had to shake off the thought of her having hopes of reconciliation; it was too hard for me to hold on to. I gently placed it in the box.

The computer completed its boot cycle and I was summoned to enter a password. Having no idea what it could be, I tried her name. I was accosted by a fast reply that the password was invalid. I tried Dana's name and it, too, was invalid. Knowing that I had no particular talent hacking into a computer, I gave up and simply clicked "Cancel." To my surprise, the system whirred into action. Damn, she had set it up so all you had to do was click cancel.

I doubled clicked on the "My Computer" icon in the top left-hand corner of the desktop and opened up "My Documents." I saw a number of folders displayed, with the names of each patient as the folder name. I gave a quick glance, not really sure why I was looking, until I ran across the name Kennard and remembered it from the caller ID. When I double-clicked it, a file in text format came up.

Marlene Kennard

04/18/01

Subject came in on employee EAP referral complaining of hopelessness. She feels guilty for husband losing his job. Husband James doesn't know she's here.

04/25/01

Subject states that she can no longer come to sessions. Very irritable. She feels husband stalking her.

05/2/01

Despite threats of terminating sessions, she shows up with bruises – fell down the stairs. Husband hasn't found work, drinking.

05/9/01

Noticeable appearance of weight loss. Jumpy and irritable. Wants to quit job but has to support husband. She has to see him through his hard times because of love.

05/16/01

Subject taking turn for worse, discouraged about life. Falling behind in bills. Exhibits signs of suicidal ideation. Gets defensive when asked about husband.

05/23/01

No call No-show.

05/30/01

Visible signs of healed bruises. Complaining of loss of sleep, thus low levels of energy. Husband trying his best.

06/06/01

Dumping on husband for not trying to find a job. When asked if he strikes her, she admits she deserves it and wallows in her preoccupation with worthlessness. Wrote prescription for Paxil 25mg.

06/13/01

Subject complaining of tiredness, but insist that she sleeps well now. Drop dosage from 25mg to 10mg.

I decided to discontinue reading patient files because I was certain that I was breaking some kind of psychotherapist-patient privacy privilege. I glanced at my watch and noticed it was approaching three. I had to finish so I could talk to the Battalion Chief. I gathered the rest of Shana's personal belongings and said my good-byes to Effie May.

By the time I arrived at the fire station for my return, the guys welcomed me back. My best buddy, Willie Ramsey, handed me a hefty envelope with nearly five thousand dollars inside from donations collected from the Local 410 Fulton County Fire Department – twenty nine fire stations in all. I was overwhelmed at the gesture. Not that I needed money. Not that I cared. Since Shana's murder occurred so soon after our divorce, she did not have time to change the insurance policy. The policy paid triple for accidental death or, in this case, murder. After funeral expenses, I had two hundred and sixty-three thousand dollars.

Ramsey had two years seniority on me. I remembered my first day on the job, Ramsey, with his large six-four frame, stood there smiling while shifting his weight from one foot to the other. I kept waiting for a rookie prank, but it never came. We established a bond, one that I never experienced with another man. After he gave me the money, I gave him a bear hug.

"You know, JT was the only brother who refused to donate," he whispered in my ear.

"Ramsey, you are always trying to stir shit up," I teased. But I knew JT had a beef with me, I just didn't know what it was. Ever since his divorce eight months ago, I noticed that he had been quite distant towards me. "Anyway, you need a haircut."

"Speaking of haircuts," Ramsey turned to me. "I gave up on being a hairstylist."

"Yeah?"

"When I started styling at Daweeds Hair Studio, man, those sisters wanted me to make their nappy roots look like Halle Barry hair."

I put my hands in my pocket and just smiled. That's all you can do with Ramsey and his part-time jobs. He originally wanted to become a fireman so that he could amass fortunes on his forty-eight-hour hiatus between shifts. His first endeavor was real estate, which fell through once he got licensed and realized that brothers wanted mansions in Buckhead but could only afford shacks in Bankhead. Then he started a degree program at Atlanta Intercontinental University, majoring in visual communications, so he could be a video production specialist making music videos for BET. He dropped out after two terms.

"What are you gonna do now?" I asked.

"The way I see it, I have four days off a week," he said as his smile took on a more serious dimension. "I'm thinking about becoming a painter."

"Ramsey, how do you go from a hairstylist to a painter?"

"Man, don't you know that you can get six hundred bucks for painting a living room?"

"Didn't know that, but how much is it gonna cost for a ladder sturdy enough to hold your big ass?"

"You ain't too far behind, Bubba."

We checked over the two fire trucks, then wound up in the kitchen. Station twenty-three was a single-level structure with the engine room separating the bunker from living quarters. The floor plan afforded us the luxury of sleep even when another fireman wanted to watch TV. The kitchen housed an industrial-sized gas burning stove and a stainless steel refrigerator. A large laminate table for eight stood between them. I went to the fridge and grabbed an orange soda and sat down.

I thought about the guys at the 23rd. We spent one fourth of our lives together and I didn't know much about any one particular fireman. In shift B, there was Ramsey, Smelly, Spoon, JT, Cap and me. Spoon always stayed out partying the day before his shift, so he normally came right in and slept until the early afternoon, unless there was a fire. JT was our resident webmaster. He updated our website constantly. Cap stayed to himself mostly. Smelly jacked off in the bathroom several times a day because he always carried a nudie magazine in there with him. I shook my head, thinking I needed to get to know these fellows more.

"I been meaning to ask you something, but at the funeral you were surrounded," Ramsey said

I looked his way.

"Have they found any suspects yet?"

I narrowed my eyes, thinking of what he said. From all the turmoil and disorder in my life I had not thought twice about justice for the murder of my wife. I had been selfish, thinking only of my pain and my feelings. What a jerk I was.

Immediately I got up and yanked the phone off the wall. Not realizing it, but I did not have the number to Detective Leicky. I held the receiver in one hand as I reached around and grabbed my wallet out of my uniform pants. When I found Leicky's card, I dialed the number.

"Homicide, Detective Leicky."

"Leicky, this is Rick Edison–"

"That's Detective Leicky. Go on."

What a smug bastard, I thought. "Have you made any arrests on my wife's murder?"

"Rick, a murder investigation is not an exact science, we have–"

"That's Mr. Edison." Two could play that game. I looked over to Ramsey who hung on every word I said. Rarely have I seen him that straight-faced.

"Look, I'm busy here. Can I help you with something?"

It came to me that he was still pissed off that I whacked him in the jaw. "How's the jaw?" I asked, suddenly realizing that I made a mistake after I heard the dial tone.

"I can't believe he hung up on me," I said more to myself than to Ramsey.

"How big of a guy is he? Maybe we can jack his ass."

"Ramsey, me and you together could jack the Atlanta Braves by ourselves."

"Oh yeah, right."

Bless his heart. Ramsey wasn't the brightest star in the sky. Sometimes he reminded me of John Coffey in the movie *The Green Mile*.

"I'll go see him in the morning when I get off."

I left the station at seven that morning, my mind set on visiting the Atlanta Police. I rushed home as others were rushing to work. The day after my shift gave me a warm feeling of relief knowing that I had the next two days off. But today I had an agenda. I planned on getting some answers from the two detectives that gave me the news of my wife's murder.

As soon as I got home, I jumped in the shower and took a hoe bath, in and out in less than two minutes. I wet my hair and put in some mousse, the black man's answer to styled hair without a stylist. As I headed for the door, dressed in slacks and a polo shirt, I heard a knock. Who would be at my door this early in the morning, I wondered.

I opened the door to see none other than Detectives Leicky and Biddings.

"Are we leaving town?" Leicky asked.

"I don't know, are you?" I asked, sarcastically.

Biddings tilted his head to one side as a puppy frequently does.

"Don't get smart, asshole," Leicky said as he pushed past me and reached for his handcuffs. "You have the right to remain silent–"

"You're arresting *me*?"

Leicky didn't respond to my question, he just continued with my Miranda rights.

Humiliated, I was escorted to the police car, the same one I rode in a few weeks ago to identify Shana's body.

5

After I went through processing, I was taken to one of the holding cells, and from what I could discern, the fourth-floor holding cell was a woman's bathroom that had been converted to four individual cells. Two feet into the tiny cell was a bunk bed with a toilet seat directly behind it. When I sat on the bed, I could touch the toilet with one hand and the bars with the other one.

The holding cell was meant for a short-term detoxification because it smelled like dried-up liquor on old carpet like the Freemont Street casinos in Vegas. I looked around, pissed off that I was *arrested* for Shana's murder.

My cellmate, a feeble white man with unruly hair and a beard that had remnants of his last meal, sat on the top bunk. When I walked in, he was speaking to his stockbroker on his cell phone, only there was no cell phone. He held his hand up to his ear like he had one of those Nokia handsets. He spoke into it and answered make-believe questions. It was absolutely amazing that the Federal Government would allow its citizens to walk around the streets of this country in a depraved mental state as his.

While in processing, I called my divorce lawyer, he said he'd have to refer me to a criminal lawyer and I yelled in the phone, conveying that I was not a criminal. He assured me that if I wanted the best representation, I needed a criminal attorney, regardless of my guilt or innocence. William Ransford showed up at the city jail for my initial consultation nearly two hours later.

We met in a small room that smelled better than my cell. I felt relieved to get away from the deranged day trader. We sat down, said our brief introductions and the first thing Ransford did was play a tape.

"This is your husband and I demand to talk to you. You can't keep putting–"

"Rick why are you calling me?" It was Shana's voice on the tape. "What do you want?"

"I want to talk about last night. Turn the answering machine off so we can talk."

"Talk? Now you want to talk? What about when I tried to talk to you

about the other women? What about that woman last night.... You know what, you don't have to explain anything. We are divorced and you can do whatever you want to whomever you want. Anyway, I have to go, I have an emergency at the hospital with one of my patients."

"Fuck your patient. I made you what you are and I can take it away–"

"Good-bye, Rick, forever."

The sound of the last conversation I had with Shana caused unsettled confusion because I didn't remember saying those punk-ass words to her. In fact, if someone had bet me my pension, I would have taken the bet and lost. I felt like shit and began to wonder if I'd be locked up for a murder I didn't commit.

"They found this in Shana's house," he said as he searched through a file, "along with your prints all over the house."

Ransford was calm and centered, enthusiasm not one of his characteristics. He wore an expensive navy blue suit with a tie the same color as his royal blue shirt.

"I lived there for seven years." I held my head in my hands. "I didn't kill her." I didn't sound convincing, not even to myself.

"I can try to talk up a deal with the DA."

"Did you hear me? I didn't kill my wife." Why was this happening to me? "When am I being arraigned?"

"This afternoon."

"Just get me out on bail." Then I thought about the money I had. "I don't want a bondsman, just pay the court whatever they ask for." I had every intention of finding out who killed Shana and I didn't want some sloppy-joe eating, police academy dropout bondsman getting ten percent of the bail for nothing.

"It might be in the seven digits because of the flight factor."

"You're my lawyer, keep it under two hundred thousand." I said matter-of-factly.

At the arraignment, Leicky and Biddings were present, sitting behind the prosecuting attorney, who looked like he just got out of college. The judge sat in a high-back cloth chair and read through what I guessed was my file. He looked up and spoke to the prosecutor.

"Counsel, a tape of an angry husband does not constitute probable cause," he said. "Until you can bring to this court reasonable suspicion, I'll have to dismiss all charges against the defendant." He turned his attention directly to the arresting officers. "I would expect you to exercise higher standards than mere suspicion and a tape to charge someone with committing a crime."

After three sentences, I felt the weight lift from my shoulders. The judicial system worked. I saw Ransford look my way for kudos, but I wasn't giving him the satisfaction. Then the judge looked at me and I felt the pressure rise again.

"As for you, Mr. Edison, you have the right to make a claim and recover damages, including attorney's fees and costs for this false imprisonment. You are free to go." He turned back to the attorney. "Counsel, I'd like to see you in my chambers."

Ramsey picked me up from the court and from there we went to Sylvia's restaurant. We took Ramsey's 4Runner and headed down Whitehall to Piedmont Avenue and then made a several left turns until we made it to Central. The smog lifted and it was turning out to be one of those topaz blue-sky days with the fluffy white clouds. I caught Ramsey up on the highlights of my morning.

"It's a scary thing that assholes can have that much power," I heard myself say.

"Man, I got a bad feeling about this one," he said.

We remained in our own thoughts for a spell.

The lunch crowd from the government buildings across from Sylvia's had not made its way, so we had our pick of seats. If you got there late, you were stuck in the banquet room where there are no windows and the small seats were too close together. We sat at a window seat and gawked at the people on their way to and from the traffic court building across the street.

Sylvia's started in Harlem as an African-American establishment that specialized in soul food. The franchise branched out to Atlanta a few years ago and put a new flavor in the south's soul food business. Once, all Atlanta offered in the way of soul food was Paschal's and Beautiful Restaurant, where you had to be some kind of Civil Rights Activist to feel comfortable. But now that Sylvia graced the new south with her slamming cornbread and greens, you could roll up your sleeves, eat with your fingers and not worry about the Ralph David Abernathy types at the next table.

Not only was the food marvelous, the atmosphere offered a mellow tone by way of the impressive Steinway in the middle of the dining area. The servers were courteous, professional and very articulate. I can't remember the last time I went to a Waffle House and my server had all her teeth.

When the server arrived with my fried pork chops, collard greens and mashed potatoes, I rubbed my hands together in anticipation of a mighty fine meal. Ramsey ordered four pieces of fried chicken, sweet potato casserole and macaroni and cheese. Our server must have known we had big appetites because she bought out an extra helping of Sylvia's sweet cornbread.

As I picked up my pork chop, Ramsey had a vacant stare.

"You mind if I ask a personal question?"

I didn't say anything.

"Where did the cops find her body?"

"They found her in one of the bio-hazardous bins at Emory Hospital."

"And you said that they have her voice on tape saying she was headed to the hospital?"

"Yeah."

Then Ramsey looked at me with one of those vacant stares. He tilted his beefy head sideways and bit his lower lip. "You ever been to Vegas?"

"Man, what the fuck is this?" I asked. "The Spanish Inquisition?"

"Answer the question. You ever been to Vegas?"

I blew out some air in contemplation at his offbeat question. "You know damn well I have."

"When you were there, did you ever look up and notice the eye in the sky?"

I sat in my despair rolling my eyes in contempt at Ramsey. Why was he talking in riddles like I was some kind of comic book collector? Then I got on his wavelength. I leaned in over the table with a sense of excitement. "The hospital might have surveillance tapes of the murder."

"Now you see."

I looked at him with that whacked pun but I gave him a big high five.

We continued eating, or rather guzzling our food when the server came over and refilled our sweet tea. Ramsey smiled every time she came by. She returned the gesture. I wondered to myself again if he would ever get married, because in my opinion, he was a nice-looking brother.

After I picked up the tab, we drove to Emory University Hospital and I formulated my plan.

Emory spent more of its grant money on research than landscaping, the campus offered no aesthetic appeal. Where I was used to tulips at my complex, this campus offered a collage of pine trees as borders high and dense as fences. The buildings had all the architectural appeal of a county jail.

We drove around until we found the security offices located behind the Carter Center for Human Rights, where we parked in the lower gate. On our way to the security building, still inside the garage, I noticed Leicky's police car.

"Son of a bitch." I stopped, not wanting to take a chance getting arrested again. "That's the detective's car.

Ramsey walked closer and peeked inside. I kept still, not sure what to do. If they caught me here, would they use it as some kind of evidence against me, like going back to the crime scene? I felt paralyzed with fear. When I glanced at Ramsey, he had opened the door, reaching in for something.

"What the hell are you doing?" I whispered. Instinctively I turned to he entrance of the security building, as a lookout, when I saw Leicky and Biddings emerge. I ran over to Ramsey, "They're coming."

We walked in a hunched-down duck squat until we were two rows behind the police car. I saw that Ramsey had a file in his hand and I gave him an 'atta-boy' wink. When we were certain that Leicky and Biddings were far from Emory, we got up from our bow and made our way into the building, not before hiding the file under the passenger seat of Ramsey's truck.

Ramsey and I entered and were immediately seized with blunt stares, the way a toddler looks at someone eating an ice cream cone. But I guessed they were on high alert since a gruesome murder occurred in their backyard.

"I'd like to speak with the head of security."

"Do you have an appointment with Mr. Leggett?" the officer asked. He was one of the few white security officers left in Atlanta, and he looked at us suspiciously.

"Do I need one?"

"Generally the Director of Security at a large University tends to have a schedule, Mr.–?"

"Edison. As in Shana Edison, who was murdered on your large University campus."

That got a rise out of him. He looked at the other guard. Lyons, a black man who wore his uniform proud, lifted the receiver and punched in four digits. As he spoke into the phone, he turned his body away from me so I was unable to hear what he said. As I waited, I turned around and saw Ramsey standing tall with his arms crossed at his chest. With a shaved head he would have looked like the black version of Yul Brynner in the *King and I.*

The black officer replaced the receiver. "Mr. Leggett will see you, briefly."

The other officer quickly produced a clipboard with an attached sign-in sheet. "You have to fill this out." I had a sense that they just wanted to shut me up.

"Will my associate need to sign in?" I said as I nodded in Ramsey's direction.

"I'm sorry, we have authorization for one, and that's you."

This is a new journey in life for me, usually I did things my way regardless of the consequences. Now I had to accept playing by someone else's rules. Or I could act like an asshole.

"You mean to tell me that my wife was brutally murdered, right here on your large university campus." I paused for effect. "And I, her husband, can't bring my representative to see the director?" The more I spoke, the louder I got. People walking by began to look. "Do I have to hire an attorney to–"

Just then, the telephone rang and Lyons picked it up. He said one word and hung up. "Have him sign in, too."

We were issued plastic laminated visitor's badges in exchange for our driver's licenses. Officer Lyons escorted us up to the fourth-floor reception lobby and left us there to wait. After a few minutes, the door to Director Leggett's office opened.

The office reminded me of a posh lawyer's suite on Peachtree Street downtown. Crown molding edged the walls of the well-appointed executive office. A large maple desk sat in front of a glass window overlooking the campus. The only difference was the security monitors – about twenty of them on the east wall, each with a thirteen-inch screen that flipped through images of the university. There was even a video feed of Emory's emergency room.

Director Leggett was downright skinny. I guessed him to be six-six and probably able to fit his entire body into one pants leg of my jeans. By looks, this lanky white man didn't have what it took to be a security director, until he spoke.

"Mr. Edison, my condolences go out to you and your family." His voice barreled throughout the room. I felt like I was back in sixth grade, and momentarily speechless. He sat behind his desk and leaned back in his executive's chair.

"Thank you." I felt nervous and didn't understand why. I felt even more ashamed knowing that Ramsey saw my uneasiness.

"What is it that I can do for you, Mr. Edison?"

What was I doing here anyway? Did I think I could just walk into this man's office and demand something? What was it that I came for?

"Mr. Leggett, I – um wanted to get a copy of the videotapes from the night my wife was murdered. I was thinking I could look them over in my spare time. I'm a fireman with two days off after each shift. I thought maybe the police missed something."

After I finished babbling, Leggett remained silent. That gave me a chance to mentally hit myself in the head for rambling like a child, *you see, I am a fireman and I have two days off after each shift. I thought maybe the police missed something.* What was I thinking?

Leggett formed a crooked smile. "Let me assure you that we at Emory and the Atlanta Police Department are working together for a resolution to this dreadful crime."

"I just wanted to –"

Leggett interrupted me by simply raising his hand. "We have complied with the request to release the video surveillance tapes to APD and together our efforts are focused on solving your ex-wife's murder."

In two words, he let me know that legally I didn't have a leg to stand on. I sat there and thought about how I was going to convince this security specialist to release the tapes to me. I stared out the window, trying to come up with something. Anything.

Then Ramsey spoke up, "Rick has declined interviews with the *Atlanta Journal-Constitution*." He looked at me. I had no idea where he was going, but it sounded better than what I had – nothing.

"Exactly." I put the ball back in his court.

"But maybe it's time to rethink the press interview. Maybe something along the lines of a large university and its lack of security." Ramsey emphasized the last words.

We turned and left.

We remained silent on the way to my apartment. I needed to see those tapes, knowing that with my free time, I could find something – anything that the detectives missed. But I was afraid Leggett saw through our bullshit. I turned to Ramsey.

"You think we can find a reporter from the *Atlanta Journal-Constitution* to write an article, or threaten to write one?" I asked, solemnly.

"I happen to know a reporter from the AJC."

"Damn, so you were telling the truth and not just crapping?" Now more excited.

"Yes and no. Let me make some calls and see a few people."

After Ramsey dropped me off to work his angle, on speculation, I drove downtown to the Atlanta Journal-Constitution. I rolled down the windows in the Expedition and played *Incognito* on the CD player. As the smooth sounds of the acid jazz filled the interior, I reflected that justice was around the corner. But something nagged at me. I turned the stereo down so I could hear myself think. Something was missing – a big piece that was right under my nose. *Think!* I exited off the highway and passed the Georgia State University campus. At first sight, it didn't appear large, but it takes up twenty-three city blocks. That's it. College campus – as in Emory University. What was Shana doing at the hospital that night? Who was she seeing? *"I have an emergency at the hospital with one of my patients."*

I grabbed my cell phone. Thankfully, Effie May answered on the second ring.

"Ms. Effie, Rick Edison here. Can you tell me who Shana– I mean Dr. Edison was seeing at the hospital the night she was murdered?" I asked, anxiously.

"Just like I told the cops, I'm not allowed to give out that information."

"But I'm trying to find out–"

"I can't even talk about this with anyone. That's what the administration told us."

"Effie, I'm her husband, dammit." I knew my emotions got the better of me as soon as I heard the words leave my mouth.

"I gotta go now." And she hung up.

Damn!

If I could find out the name of the patient, I might have a viable lead. I thought about turning around and asking one of the nurses to help me. Women flirted with me constantly, and this time, maybe it could turn into something productive. Then I thought about it in depth. What would I say, *give me a list of all patients that night*? Too many things at once – Leggett and the tapes, my arrest. My head started throbbing, so I focused on the drive and continued on MLK until I reached Marietta.

The AJC building was located on Marietta Street in the old section of downtown where four-story office buildings still reigned. It was a nine-story, sand-dusted brick structure on a gravel covered cobblestone street. Some of the cobblestone showed through weathered pavement. A multitude of non-English-speaking merchandise vendors and peddlers milled the streets, and before I entered the building I bought a purse for Dana and gave ten bucks to a homeless woman pushing her three kittens down the sidewalk in a Kroger cart.

After September 11th, corporate America had armed its reception desks with more guards. The AJC was no exception. There were two sisters manning the desk, wearing uniforms from Pennington Security Services. And as far as I could tell, they couldn't chase a criminal two blocks without keeling over from a coronary.

"Hello, ladies, I was wondering if I could get a list of reporters that work here?"

One of the ladies, LaRonda, almost pushed her co-worker to the side so she could talk to me. "We don't have that kind of information, but if you give me a name of a reporter, I could call them and see if they will let you up."

"I don't have a name. That's why I wanted a list."

She just shrugged.

"Thank you for your time, Miss LaRonda."

I don't know what I was looking to gain from the visit, so I left, gearing myself up for the onslaught of financially challenged people begging for change. I looked the other way this time. After exiting the building, a sign on the second floor of the building across the street caught my attention. *For Rent* – posted in the window of an old four-story, brick building. The building storefront was an old shoe repair shop. Next to it was Mandarin Gardens Chinese Restaurant. When I crossed the street, I saw smaller lettering on the sign, handwritten, asking to inquire within.

The shoe repair shop smelled of leather and something else, a funky smell that reminded me of Frito-Lays corn chips. The place looked like an exhibition in a Civil War museum. Inside, a large Stanley Bostitch buffer machine the color of a John Deer backhoe stood in the center of the dim room. A large wooden counter separated it from the public. The counter had six worn stools in front of it, as if it were some kind of shoe-bar. An older black man in with nappy gray hair stood at the machine working on a pair of high-heeled boots. He wore a stained apron stretched tightly around his round belly. When I made a purposeful noise with my keys, he turned to me.

"Hey son, what can I do you for?"

I gave him my name and mentioned the sign. "I'd like to take a look at the office."

"Well, I wouldn't call it an office, per se." He chuckled to himself and as he did, his belly jiggled. He wiped his hands on his apron and offered it to me. "I'm Doc Jones, people just call me Doc." He grabbed some keys from underneath the counter and made his way around the to the side I stood. "It's more like a room with a beat-up couch and an old desk rather than an office."

"I'd still like to see it if I can."

Doc Jones exuded some kind of inner peace that I don't see in a lot of people and I was drawn to him. I followed him to the front door, where he turned the "Closed" sign around to face the street, then he unlocked another door I had not noticed when I entered the shop. Doc moved slowly up the dingy stairway, floorboards creaking under our weight. He held on tightly to the handrails and they squeaked as well. The place was ten degrees warmer than outside and it smelled like a mixture of urine and sweat.

"This old building been good to me. This room is the only vacancy I have. Pretty decent long-term tenants I got."

"Any apartments?"

"No, sir. Just business tenants. I would have had to get a whole different set of inspections to rent it as a multi-family dwelling."

We made it to the second-floor landing and Doc Jones paused to catch his breath. "Here we are."

He unlocked a wooden door that had a frosted privacy pane. It reminded me of one of those offices that private investigators used like in Dick Tracey movies.

Doc Jones must have read my mind. "Rented this place to a private detective named Mike Arnold. Stayed in this one room for nearly ten years."

"What happened to him?"

"Dunno."

The room was a thirteen-by-seventeen box. Directly opposite the door, two floor-to-ceiling windows, with a desk between them, overlooked the street. On the wall were silhouettes of picture frames, outlined by ten years of cigarette smoke. The floor was thinly carpeted, no padding underneath. And adjacent to the desk was a worn sofa, which I liked right away. It was wine-red leather and brass-tacked. I did a three-sixty, taking it all in.

"I normally let this go for three hundred bucks a month, but since I'm getting up there in age and can't get around to painting it, I'll let it go for two fifty."

I signed the month-to-month lease, and as we spoke, down in the shoe shop again, I told him that my wife had died recently and that extra space felt lonely. He gave me some grandfatherly advice and told me to stay busy, no matter what. That's what I planned on doing. Staying busy, finding the sick fuck who murdered my wife. I didn't say that to Doc Jones, though.

I drove home, worried that Leggett would not give up the tapes. I had to find a way to convince him that giving them up was the best option. But what did he have to lose if he denied us? I had to find a plan. When I passed a billboard boasting BellSouth's Complete Choice package, a plan came to mind. I called Aisha and called in yet another favor. When I hung up with her, satisfied that my efforts were coming into focus, I made it home and fell asleep watching television.

When I woke up the next morning, I felt as though I slept for weeks. I didn't have a hangover, nor was I rushing from a strange woman's bedroom. It was a new feeling for me, and a good one. I wanted to see Dana, but it was too hard right now. I spoke to her every night on the telephone, and last night's conversation had been especially hard when she asked when was her mommy coming home from heaven. My heart sank and all I could think to tell her was her mother was waiting on her to get there.

How could someone take a mother away from a child?

A few days passed and everything was falling into place. I went to work and shortly after we punched in, the guys at the station were into their own thing. Business as usual at the 23rd. Ramsey was in the kitchen, cooking up some scrambled eggs with cheese, Bob Evans sausage and fried potatoes with onions. Hailing from Cleveland, he hooked me on those fried potatoes and I wish more restaurants served them. He told me that in the Midwest, potatoes were to them what grits were to people like me from the South. Between us, we could go through a ten-pound sack of them in one sitting.

It was an unwritten rule that whoever cooked had to make enough for everyone. Another rule – the cook never washed the dishes, so after every meal, we played gin rummy, with the loser cleaning the kitchen. While we ate, I told him about the activities of the other day.

"Why did you rent an office? Don't you have a second bedroom at your apartment?"

"I want to get those tapes from Leggett."

Ramsey looked at me questioningly. I walked over the wall phone and punched in Doc Jones' number at the shoe shop. When I conveyed my message, I hung up and smiled.

"Hell you smiling for?" he said in between bites.

I didn't answer. Then his cell phone rang. He looked at the caller ID and then at me.

"This is the reporter from the paper."

"How do you know?" I asked, trying to hold in my laughter.

"Cause it says so." He turned the LCD screen around so I could see the "AJC" name flashing.

"Answer it, before they hang up."

Ramsey answered the phone in his best impression of proper English, going as far as to lift his chin like some European, biscotti-eating chum. He looked at me, serious at first, then he handed me the phone.

I turned so Ramsey wouldn't see me laughing. "Thanks, Doc. I owe you one."

Ramsey, in his disgust, got up from the table and emptied the remaining contents on his plate. "Why are you over there playing games?"

"Stay with me, Rambo. Leggett is director of security at Emory, right?"

"That's right."

"And being a director of security over a large university gives him access to special security measures and counter measures, right? Now, when someone calls from the office, Leggett's caller ID will say "AJC," as in my new company name, Atlanta Janitorial Company.

He laughed. "That's some good thinking, man. I bet you never guess who I saw at Daweeds."

"The reporter for the AJC?"

"None other. Kimisha Lawton, and she agreed to meet you."

The alarm went off. Lights flashed as the deafening bell interrupted our conversation and put us into high gear. I ran to the locker room and threw on my turnout gear. In less than a minute, the men of the 23rd were loaded in the ladder and headed out. Cap rode in the passenger seat as JT drove. JT rated engineer so he was our driver and Ramsey was his backup in case he was on a scheduled off day. Some weeks we worked more than forty hours, signifying a union-authorized scheduled off day, or SOD. Therefore, in any given month, each fire fighter has a SOD, amounting to a five-day break. This system worked but not too well, because if JT and Ramsey both took vacation during the same week, my classification would jump from fire fighter two to driver/engineer. Sometimes I didn't feel comfortable barreling down a busy street in a big ladder.

We arrived at the fire, a burning car in Mountain Grove Apartments on Candler Road. After we extinguished the blaze, final investigations determined that the vehicle was stolen, dumped at the apartment complex and set afire to hide latent fingerprints. We headed back to the station and showered to get the smoke out of our clothes and hair. Even though it was fire, we considered it a good fire because no one was hurt.

I sat on the couch opposite Spoon, who wore his hangover like a bad habit. He slouched on the sofa with his head lying on the armrest and stared into the television watching *Blind Date*, with every other fireman in Atlanta.

"Spoon, let me ask you something."

"Can't you see I'm trying to sleep?"

"Maybe you should lay off the booze for a while," I said, more out of concern than superiority.

Matthew Witherspoon was a short brother compared to me, but he was thick like Tyson. He wore his hair in a low-cut fade and always managed to have it lined up. To my knowledge, he's never been married. "Do you and your brother still do contracting work on the side?"

He shifted and turned his body away from me. "Yeah, every now and then."

"I need some work done and wanted to know if you'd do it."

"Just let me know and I'll talk it over with my brother."

"I'm willing to pay scale."

I got his attention then. He heaved his body up from the slouched position and turned to look at me. "Which scale are you talking about, union or contractor?"

"Union."

"Now we can talk. What you got going on?"

"I just rented a place on Marietta, about four blocks down from MARTA and–"

"You know what MARTA stands for?" Spoon interrupted.

"Metropolitan Atlanta Rapid Transit Authority, why?"

"It really means Moving African-Americans Rapidly Through Atlanta, since it ain't nothing but a bunch of us who ride it anyway. You know Five Points MARTA station sits in exactly the same spot where Atlanta's only slave market used to be back in 1853?"

The guy was smart, he just needed to have it coaxed out of him.

I explained to him that my single-room office needed a paint job and some new carpet and after I gave him the dimensions, he said he'd charge me a flat rate of two grand. It seemed a bit high, but money was not a problem at the moment. Our old house sold in less than two weeks. With Shana buying mortgage insurance, I was sitting on nearly a half million dollars.

I spent the next day with Dana, and tried my best to keep her mind occupied with books and toys. I know I was on the verge of spoiling her too much, because whatever she asked for, I got it. Aisha was doing a great job keeping her in check by not giving in to her every whim, but it was hard for me.

On my second off day, I arranged for the Goodwill to collect every piece of furniture and clothing that was in the house. I couldn't bear to see, touch or smell the memories of our past lives together. With an empty house, a spoiled kid and a new office, I was ready to go over the sting with Ramsey and Kimisha from the *Atlanta Journal-Constitution*.

6

The *Atlanta Journal-Constitution* reporter, Kimisha Lawton, called to set up a meeting. Hearing her soft and sweet voice reminded me of Shana when things were going well. We agreed to meet at the Wall Street Deli in the Equitable building downtown. I gave her my description and she said to order her a tuna sandwich on a croissant roll and she'd find me. I had never been at the deli, but when I saw how packed the place was, I looked forward to seeing what the hoopla over the food was about.

I ordered a Boars Head turkey sandwich on sourdough bread with onions, lettuce, tomatoes, extra mayo and cucumbers. I had no idea why I chose cucumbers, but I thought I'd try them since several folks ahead of me put them on their sandwiches. After I bit into my sandwich, a gorgeous woman came and sat at my bistro table. From my point of view, she had to be five ten with long sandy brown hair, worn in a fashionable wrap style. She was Manhattan-shopper-chic in an impressive navy blue Rena Rowan pantsuit with a starched white blouse. I wiped the mayonnaise from the corner of my mouth.

"Hi Rick, I'm Kimi." She offered her hand to me.

"Hello – I um. Here's your sandwich."

Here's your sandwich. What a dork thing to say. Her hands felt so smooth and firm. Most women that looked that good starved themselves and it showed in their frail, bony hands. But Kimi's hands had substance. She must have been a size fourteen, maybe sixteen, but with her height, she looked no bigger than a ten.

"Thank you. How much do I owe you?"

"No please, it's on me. If I'm lucky, I hope you say those same words to me when we finish."

She looked at me as if I had called her a nappy head cunt. "No no no. What I mean is, I need a favor and I'd be willing to pay."

She let out a breath. And so did I.

I took a deep breath and briefed her on my situation. "They found her body in a Dumpster at Emory Medical Center."

"I am so sorry to hear that. It must have been awful," she said with such a genuine concern that I had to pause so my eyes wouldn't well up.

"To make a long story short, the Atlanta Police Department arrested me, only to have it thrown out by the judge. I need to find some justice. I asked the Director of Security at Emory to–"

"Dan Leggett?"

"How do you know him?"

"I'm a reporter, remember." She played with her sandwich. "He's a tough man. I've heard stories."

I wiped my mouth, very aware of the extra mayo. If I only knew she was going to be this gorgeous and not some kind of frog lady, I would've got a regular helping.

"I just want to see the surveillance tapes of the day she was murdered."

"And where do I fit into this plan?"

She was sharp. I explained to her about the Atlanta Janitorial Company, the office directly across the street from the real AJC and the article she was supposedly going to write on my human-interest story. She stared out in reflection.

"What's in it for me?"

"I'd be willing to pay. Just name the price."

Kimisha took her time with her thoughts. I decided not to invade. Besides, she didn't look easily manipulated. A sparked desire stirred in me and I looked away to shake it off. Why is it that I feel I'm entitled to a woman's attention, and when threatened by any form of rejection, it turns into a sexual obsession? She looked at me, thoughtfully.

"Here's the deal, I will go along with your tryst, if and only if you give me the exclusive story on any developments."

"Developments?" I asked.

She looked at her watch and took control of her sandwich situation. "If you find the killer."

"You'll write a story on that?"

"Oh, you have no idea how fast I'll write a story on it. Think in headlines, Rick, 'Grieving Husband Nabs Wife's Killer.'"

I guess I hadn't thought of it that way. Maybe that's why Leggett and the detectives were not willing to help me help them. A headline of that potency wouldn't look good for them. I made a mental note to start thinking in headlines.

She folded her napkin, reached in her purse for money and attempted to pay me but I grabbed her hand. I noticed that she pulled back from my touch.

"Please let me pay."

She thought about this.

"Ok. Just don't let it happen again." When she smiled her cute nose rose up ever so slightly.

I admired a woman willing to pay, not just faking the jump. But I got the sense from Kimi that she really wanted to.

We set up the call for the next day at my new office. She left, giving me her business card with her home number.

We agreed to meet at Mandarin Gardens, the Chinese restaurant next to Doc Jones' shoe joint. Ramsey and I sat at one of the small tables waiting for Kimi to walk over from the AJC across the street. The owner saw us walk in, only to take up of one the restaurant's only two tables.

"You sit, you buy," he said in broken English.

Ramsey ordered the deep fried ribs with red bean sauce and I got the house special – fried rice with shrimp, chicken, beef and pork. For a dumpy hole in the wall place, the food was the bomb. We were cleaning off our plates when she walked in.

She took one look around the place. "You notice any stray cats outside?" Kimi asked when she saw us eating.

I immediately grabbed my coke and swallowed the rest of the contents. Ramsey sat there and licked his fingers.

"If it taste like chicken, then it's all right with me."

"Just kidding. Can we get started? I have a deadline."

We walked up the dank stairwell with me taking the lead. Since I saw Kimi the first time, I took some time to spruce up the place. I purchased a nicer desk that I picked up from Office Depot, and while I was there, bought a computer, printer, fax, scanner and any other gadget that the stringy hair salesperson informed me I needed. I even bought one of those twenty-seven-inch flat screen televisions with the built-in VCR just in case Leggett caved and gave us the tapes. The telephone I purchased had all the bells and whistles and, as I was told, was equipped to handle IP traffic, whatever that meant.

I decided to keep the old couch.

The smell of fresh paint and new carpet took the place of the musty smell of stale cigarette smoke and for that, the two grand I paid Spoon was well worth it. Kimi headed to the couch and I stopped her.

"Why don't you sit at the desk? You know, to get into character."

"I am a reporter, that's what I *do*."

I remained silent, no need for me to top the *Here's your sandwich* line I blundered. She walked to the other side of the desk and Ramsey caught me looking at her backside. I felt ashamed. How could I look at another woman when the last time I saw my wife, her lifeless body lay on a cold metal table?

I shook it off and broke the silence.

"Here's the number right here." I moved the business card that I swiped from Leggett's desk. She looked at it.

"Ready?" she asked.

"Let's rock."

She lifted the receiver and punched in the numbers. I sat on the leather couch and felt nervous as a declawed cat in a room full of rats.

"Yes, I'm Kimisha Lawton with the *Atlanta Journal-Constitution*. I'd like to speak with Director Leggett."

There was a moment of silence as she held the phone.

"Oh, I see. Yes. Tell him that I am writing a story on the Shana Edison murder, from the widower's point of view, and I was calling to give Mr. Leggett a chance to comment on the accusations."

She paused and I stopped breathing.

"Yes, I can." Kimi covered the mouthpiece and pantomimed that the other person put her on hold. I held up my fingers in an *OK* position while she seemed to stare right through me. I wondered to myself what she was thinking.

"Yes. I'd like to speak with Director Leggett." She looked surprised. "Oh this is? I'm Kimisha Lawton with the AJC and I'd like to get your comment before we run a story on the Shana Edison murder."

There was an awkward moment of silence. I felt my hand grab the edge of the sofa in anticipation.

"Yes, I can." And then she hung up the phone.

I stared at her. My narrow ribbon of hope rested with the acquisition of those tapes. And now I had nothing – no other leads or angles to pursue the marauder who killed my wife. I felt like a nomad wandering in a waterless existence. "What happened?" I asked dejectedly.

"He asked if I can wait one day on the story, then he'd give me his comment."

"What does that mean?" Ramsey asked the very question I was going to ask.

"It could mean several things." She stood up and paced nervously. "It could mean that he's calling my boss to check my status, in which case, I'm up that proverbial creek."

"Or?"

"Or it could mean that he wants to check this phone line. Are you sure it comes up AJC on the caller ID?"

"Yes," I said as I lowered my head. What made me think that I could outsmart a director of security? He probably had years of tactical training, years of real life experience and the intuition of a woman. If he found out and informed Leicky and Biddings, I could be in some serious legal trouble.

"What's your cell phone number?"

"My cell phone number?"

"Yes, what's the number?"

I gave it to her and understood that she was going to call my cell phone so she could see the caller ID. When it rang, I simply answered it.

"Yeah," I said in a drab voice, thinking it was Kimisha. Listening half-heartedly to the voice on the other, I noticed that her mouth wasn't moving. I jumped up. My heart raced wilder than a feral cat. It was Leggett. "Um yes, OK. Thanks."

"That was Leggett. He said if I nix the story, he'll give me a copy of the tapes." I turned off the phone and went to Kimi and gave her a big bear hug. I gave Ramsey a big high five. The thrill and excitement that I felt at that moment were unparalleled to any accomplishment I had in my life. It really worked.

Kimi left us there to stare at the newly painted walls. I looked out one of the windows and watched her as she sashayed across the street. She was a smooth and elegant creature that only God could have made. Ramsey saw this.

"Man, you are incredible. How can you think of another woman at a time like this?"

"Thanks for being a good friend," I said sarcastically. "I'm lonely, I'm horny and this is the first time in a very long while I don't have the warmth of a woman in my life."

"Welcome to the real world, Casanova."

"Shut the fuck up before I put my foot in your big black ass."

"You think *my* ass is big? Ought to take a look at yours."

I couldn't help but to laugh, in spite of myself. No matter what he and I went through, Ramsey was a good sport who took my sarcasm, letting it roll off his shoulders.

In a short time I grew restless, sitting there in that box of an office staring out the window. "Hey Rambo, what say we go to Dugan's and celebrate?"

"Sounds like a plan to me."

We drove to Dugan's Tavern on Ponce de Leon instead of the one in Stone Mountain. It was the museum of all bars, offering more in the way of characters. One time when I was in college I partied there, and caught a show. Some transient lady beat the shit out of her husband, right there in the bar. Since then, bouncers roam the place on weekends to weed out the flagrant who slip in from next door.

The bar sits next to the Clermont Logde, a cheesy motel housing fugitives and transients, forced to live in sub-human shelter. They offer rates anywhere between hourly and monthly. There was a bar in the motel that dubbed as a strip joint on Friday and Saturday nights. Once when I was drunk, I visited the strip joint and couldn't believe the sight of the less-than-shapely women who actually took their clothes off and danced for money. I offered to give them money to put their clothes back on.

Atlanta's late-afternoon searing heat robbed me of my precious body fluids. My shirt felt sticky even though air was blowing full blast in my Expedition. I pulled into the parking lot with Ramsey tailing. We entered the establishment and the relief of the air-conditioning was a welcome respite. We grabbed two seats at the center bar and ordered beers, Lighthouse for me and Budweiser for him. To this day, I don't know why anybody drinks Bud – it makes my head pound and tastes like recycled piss. When our drinks arrived, I took a long swig and noticed a lone patron at the other end enjoying the solace of his drink. My drink went down so smooth and welcoming that I wondered if I might be an alcoholic. Ramsey sat there twirling his bottle around like it was going to change the awful taste or something.

"Thanks for help, especially with Kimi," I said, taking another swallow of my beer. I motioned for the bartender to bring another one. I calculated that by the time he reached into the cooler, popped open the cap and walked it down to me, I'd be finished with the first one.

"No problem, man." He paused then turned and looked at me. "Rick, let me ask you a personal question."

"Shoot."

"What are you going to do if you find something on the tapes?"

I stared across the bar and something struck me as strange about the patron. It was ninety degrees outside and he wore one of those 'Members Only' jackets that were popular in the eighties. Two things I saw that were wrong about him, one, why have on a jacket with the temperature being so high. And two, if you have to wear a jacket, never ever wear the played-out 'Members Only'. Ramsey stared at me. "I just want to see if those two detectives missed anything."

"How would you know what to look for?"

"I plan to look at everything. It's worth a shot, besides I have nothing but time to hunt down the sadistic sonabitch."

Ramsey had that far-off stare I'd seen recently on Kimi. Was I beginning to provoke people in some sort of deep philosophical reflection?

"I – something has been wearing on me about this whole thing, and I can't put my finger on it. It's something so close and we don't even know it."

Just then, a scraggly woman wearing a black skullcap walked in and headed toward us.

"Dis seat taken?" she asked Ramsey, slurring.

Ramsey just looked at her and turned back to me without saying word.

She sat down, pulling a cigarette from her bra. She wore a long sleeve tan blouse with jeans at least one size too large. I immediately surmised that she was either a heroine junkie or a crack ho. "Got a light?"

"Don't smoke," he said without looking, trying to ignore the jean-clad skeleton.

"Can you at least buy me a drink?"

Ramsey turned and looked at her. "If I buy you a drink, will you go sit at the other side of the bar?"

"Sure, honey, whatever gets your rocks off."

I had to put my head down and smile. Sometimes poverty wasn't enough to wipe away vanity. Out of the corner of my eye I saw Members Only rise out of his stool, headed toward us. He walked up to the back of Ramsey and poked him on the shoulder to get his attention.

"Ay man, don't go messin' wit my little woman."

He was drunker than a sailor on a twenty-four-hour liberty.

Ramsey chuckled to himself and motioned for the bartender. When he arrived, he gave him a five-dollar bill.

"Get this lady a drink and serve it to her over there." He pointed to the space where the man came from.

"Can I just have the five spot instead of the drink?"

"Whatever gets your rocks off," Ramsey said and smiled again.

Suddenly the man grabbed Ramsey's forearm. "I said don't be messin' with my woman."

"You better get your scrawny paws off me or I'll see to it that you won't be messing with your own woman."

"Oh, what you gonna do, take her from me?"

I know alcohol generates some kind of liquid courage, but I had no idea it gave a man that much audacity. Ramsey was twice his size, at least. I felt the need to warn the man. "You might want to go back to your seat," I offered my two cents, for what it was worth.

"Was I talking to you, tar baby?"

This dude must have been on some kind of hallucinogen because those were fighting words, but I decided to let it go instead of rearranging his jaw. Actually it was kind of funny because being that I was as dark as Wesley Snipes, I have been called everything from Kunta to Kingsford charcoal, but never a tar baby.

The bartender placed the five bucks Ramsey had given him back on the counter. "Why don't y'all take the money and leave?" He said to the couple.

"I ain't leaving until Bubba here atpologizes to me."

"It's apologize, you brain-dead bastard."

Members Only pointed directly in Ramsey's face. "Never again call me a bastard."

I guess my good ole' friend Rambo had as much as he could take from this bottom feeder because he swiftly grabbed the finger that pointed in his face, bent it in the direction opposite of what God had intended and stood up. The man got down on bent knees and whined like the coward that he was. Ramsey snatched him up by his neck and threw him out of the bar like he owned the place. The woman grabbed the five dollars and ran after her man. Ramsey looked at the bartender, wondering if he crossed the line.

He finished drying a glass. "Drinks on the house, gentlemen." He smiled at Ramsey. "Anytime you want a part-time job as a bouncer, just let me know."

We stayed there drinking beers until rush hour had long passed. Sitting at the bar drinking for hours had its disadvantages. When I rose to leave, my body wanted to stay. The barstool acted like a magnetic force, capturing me in is powerful field like a current-carrying conductor. I stumbled back in my seat and took a few deep breaths to get the strength to pull up. I said my good-byes to Ramsey and reminded him that we had to start our shift at seven a.m.

I got in the Expedition, and for some unknown reason I laughed out loud. I laughed so hard I had to grab the steering wheel to keep from convulsing. When I came around, I decided to take Ponce de Leon to Stone Mountain instead of jumping on the interstate. Ponce turns into Lawrenceville Highway. That was a mistake. No sooner than I had gotten out of Midtown, driving through the narrow street where the old style plantation homes still stood, the DeKalb Police turned on their blue lights for my occasion. I wasn't laughing then. As a fireman, it was imperative that we maintained a clean driving record because the department checks the DMV record once a year.

After I pulled over, the officer took his merrily time getting out of the patrol car. I sat there and smiled, thinking of those blue lights. They reminded me of the times my grandmother took us to K-Mart for those Blue Light specials. She wandered around until the announcement came over the PA system, then we had to rush to the blue lights. I felt embarrassed back then, but now the joy and pangs I feel when I think of those bittersweet memories serve to remind me how good life was back then. The officer finally made his way to my truck.

"Do you know why I stopped you?"

I could not control my laughter. "Shouldn't you know why you stopped me?" After the words and the subsequent laughter left my mouth, I instinctively knew it was the wrong thing to say.

"Oh, we have a smart-ass. Let me see your license and insurance."

As I fumbled through my wallet, the officer shined his flashlight at my every move. My imminent doom seemed very realistic as I had trouble sliding the laminated driver's license out of the slit. When I finally released it, my work badge fell out. I handed him the ID instead of my license and insurance card. He grabbed it without looking.

"You a fireman?"

"Yes."

"What local?"

"Local 410, Fulton County, station twenty-three," I said, giving him more information than he asked for.

The officer looked up at the night sky as if he were trying to decide something. When I saw him radio in a single-car backup, I knew I was headed straight for jail. Instead, the other officer who joined us, with his blue lights flaring, asked me to get out. He jumped in my car as the first officer led me to the front seat of his car. I got a police-driven escort to my apartment. Both officers shook my hand when we made it to my place and informed me to get a designated driver when I went out drinking. I guess the tragedy that befell my fellow co-workers in New York on September 11th opened the door for respect for our chosen livelihoods.

7

When I woke the next morning, I felt like someone stuffed my mouth full of cotton and plugged my saliva glands. I felt extremely dehydrated. My face felt puffy and my breath smelled like a prison shit can. I got in the shower and stayed there until my skin pruned. I made it into work and sat at the kitchen table with a cup of coffee and a Coke. I needed the coffee to keep me up and I needed the coke to fend off dehydration. Spoon stood over the stove cooking that good Hormel Black Label bacon and scrambled eggs with cheese.

"Hey man, I wanted to thank you for giving me that job," he said.

"No problem. You did a good job."

"Thanks." He fixed a plate and sat across from me at the table. "I met your landlord, Doc Jones. He's something else."

"Yeah, good people."

"Can you imagine going from being a doctor to a shoe repairman? "

Something wasn't right about this, but I couldn't place it.

Spoon took in a forkful of eggs. "Rick, Doc Jones offered me more work than I could possibly handle. I may need to hire some Mexicans to help me." He paused and looked at me with bright eyes. "He said he has a lot of doctor friends that may need some remodeling. I want to thank you for setting me up like that. I feel like I have a goal and not some drunk trying to make it off the coattails of my brother." He looked away, fighting off tears

"You'll be all right."

"I went to a couple of AA meetings too. Sober now for three whole days."

That was it. Spoon was actually up and about as opposed to sleeping all day like he normally did.

"Man, after last night, I may need to go a meeting with you."

"Come on."

I thought about those words and pondered the thought of going to a meeting with him. Alcohol never helped me accomplish anything. In fact, every time I got in trouble with other women, alcohol played into the equation.

I spent the rest of the day sleeping and eating. I didn't realize that I forgot to eat last night and after my first nap, my stomach let me know. Ramsey made a killer beef stew, and even in the middle of summer, it was good. Fortunately, we didn't get an alarm that entire day and I had time to think about my plan. Leggett didn't tell me how I was to get the tapes. Did he expect me to come get them or was he going to mail them to me? All I knew was that I wanted to thoroughly look them over.

When my shift ended the next morning, I went home feeling better than the day before. I jumped in the shower with no immediate plans. While I lathered up, I heard a pounding at the door. I had to leave the shower with a towel wrapped around my lower torso. I peeked through the peephole and saw Lyons, from Emory security, standing on the other side. He held a medium-sized box.

I opened the door.

"How did you know where I lived?" I asked as I caught him looking at my bare chest.

"We're in the security business, that's what we do."

He handed me the box and simply walked away. What a smug bastard, *We're in the security business, that's what we do.* Why is it that everyone wants to tell me what they do, like I don't already know.

I called Ramsey and told him that I was on my way to the office to view the tapes.

The traffic was pretty heavy for nine in the morning, especially eastbound to downtown. Today I didn't mind because of all the activity. With the tapes I was certain we could come up with a lead. Something ate at my insides about them. I felt ambivalent about looking into the gruesome scene that I was sure would be visible. I didn't know if I was ready. Once on King Drive, my thoughts were so disorientated I missed my turn and had to circle back around to get on Marietta.

Doc Jones stood out front sweeping the debris from the previous night. As I drove the block looking for a parking space, I saw him talking to a vagrant. I got the impression that he liked to talk, no matter who was in his present company. Vendors across the street began putting up their red and blue striped tents and hooking merchandise on the mesh wiring attached to the tent poles. Employees dashed in the glass-boxed buildings that surrounded the area and smells of the city emitted from the boroughs of the underground sewage and drainage infrastructure.

I grabbed the box and headed toward my office. There in the center of Marietta Street stood a century-old statue of Henry Grady, a celebrated journalist for the *Atlanta Journal*, whose major credit was the visionary of the *New South*. He advocated an end to the tumultuous era of hatred following the Civil War, even though his own father was struck and killed by a Yankee bullet. I felt the need to salute him, but my hands were compromised.

Doc Jones stopped me before I could get the key out. I was hoping to slide past him without interaction.

"Hey man, I met your partner, Mathew Witherspoon," he said.

I wanted to tell him that he was just a co-worker but I decided to let it go.

"Yeah, he does good work." I place the box down so I could reach in my jeans and get the key. I wanted to get upstairs and watch the tapes.

"I'm gonna hire him to do some more work around here." He paused and rubbed his round belly. "I got to thinking, this place probably hadn't been remodeled since the Federal Reserve sold it in sixty-nine."

That got my attention. "The Federal Reserve was in this building?"

"Sure was," Doc said as he looked up and admired his building.

"Well, maybe I'll drill some holes in the walls and try to find some stashed cash," I said after I found my keys and opened the door.

"Whatever you find, I get half."

"I didn't know we were married." I smiled and entered the building. Before I got two feet in, Doc peeked his head in the doorway. I just couldn't break away from him.

"I've been meaning to ask you something," he paused, making me more anxious. "A couple of days ago, I saw someone taking pictures of this building." Do you think Mathew was taking pictures, you know, to ad to his portfolio?"

"I'll ask him. Did you get a good look at the man?"

"Funny thing is, I couldn't tell if it was a man or woman. When I tried to get closer to find out, they sped off."

"I'll ask."

"Ok, son, don't be a stranger."

When I heard that word, guilt came over me like a huge wave from a roiling sea. I felt a quintessential feeling of fondness when he referred to me as 'son', as it was a welcomed term of endearment.

I sat down at my desk and I got a whiff of a sweet fragrance. I sniffed again and remembered it was the perfume that Kimi wore. Just then, Ramsey walked in with a bothered look.

"What's up?" I asked while gently removing the VHS tapes from the box like they were some kind of ancient Egyptian artifacts.

"I can't get rid of creepy feeling." He studied each tape as I pulled it out. "I've been thinking, maybe we ought to let the police handle this."

"The police think *I* did it, remember." I stopped, placed a hand on my waist and turned to face him. "Why the sudden change, Rams?"

"I don't know. I'm just scared of what we'll find."

I reached in the box and pulled out the last videotape. I studied it closely. It was a plain tape with no markings on them, no labels or any numbers. For a week, the tapes consumed every thought and most of my actions. Now that I had the physical tapes, the anticipation outweighed the objective. But my chest tightened when I imagined the actual murder. *Would it be on tape?*

I grabbed one, put it in the VCR and pressed play. We stood around the TV screen, holding our breath like we watching a resuscitation of a prize-winning gamecock.

Then the screen glowed a vivid blue and divided into four separate color images, each showing individual video feeds of the hospital. Undoubtedly Emory spent big bucks on surveillance. In the upper right hand quadrant, we were looking down on an entrance area where a sliding glass door opened and an older white gentleman entered. Closer examination revealed a clerk manning an information desk. Some people stopped to inquire about something or another while other people that entered through the motion censored doors walked on by.

On the upper left-hand quadrant, there was a monitored hallway. The lower right quadrant displayed the emergency room admissions and the last quadrant revealed a ward in the hospital itself. On the bottom of the screen, I saw the date and time stamp on the left-hand side. It was the morning of Shana's murder. Instinctively, I gasped for air. I was so engrossed that when I went to sit down, I almost missed my seat, landing on the arm rail. I heard something crack like splintered wood. When I turned to see, I had cracked the plastic casing in back of the arm rail. I guess it wasn't designed to withstand my body weight. I continued watching in silence as the four quadrants played on the screen simultaneously, until, unbelievably, I fell asleep.

Ramsey's snoring woke me as I looked over to the couch where he slept. I felt somewhat disappointed with myself. The time stamp on the monitor told me that I slept for nearly two hours. I must have shuffled too loudly because Ramsey stirred and woke up.

"This is grueling, man," he said as he wiped a line of drool from the side of his cheek.

"Why don't you go home, I'll stay and watch the rest of this one?"

"Are the rest of the tapes the same?" he asked as he pointed to the stack of tapes on the desk.

Ramsey posed a good question. If all the tapes showed in simulcast, the task of searching for clues would be arduous. I reached down, grabbed a random tape and replaced it with the first tape. The vision on the screen was exactly the same as the first one, four quads playing at the same time. I did some quick calculations – six tapes multiplied by four camera angles each gave us twenty-four different views of the day Shana was murdered. I felt good knowing that I could give more effort filtering through every camera angle, than the cops or Emory, but it wasn't going to be easy.

Then Ramsey shifted his gaze from the TV screen to me and smiled.

"I'm about to make you a happy man, but it's gonna cost you."

"If you can make this easier to view, I'll pay whatever it takes," I said pinching the bridge for my nose. "Whatcha' got?"

"Remember when I went to school at AIU?"

"I can't keep up with your get-rich-quick scheme of the month. What's AIU?"

"Atlanta Intercontinental University. I only stayed two quarters but when I was there, I saw some students about to graduate working on a video like that." Ramsey pointed to the split screen. "I went over and asked how they compiled four video feeds into one screen and they told be about the Avid Media Composer. It's an editing machine that can do all kinds of shit."

I rubbed my chin, thinking about the editing machine he told me about. "You said it took four different video feeds and channeled them into one screen, but can it take one feed and split them into four separate sources?"

"I don't know, but my guess is it can."

I rose out of my chair, ready to leave. "Let's go to Best Buy and get one."

"Man, you can't walk into a low-end electronics retail shop and pick up an AMC. You have to order one through a trade magazine or go a specialty shop to buy one."

I walked closer to him. "I can't wait to order this AMV–"

"It's AMC, Avid Media Composer," he corrected me.

"Whatever. Who are you now, the next Spike Lee?" I asked, annoyed that he had the balls to correct me.

"What's wrong, man, you can't stand it when someone knows more than you? That's probably why you cheated on Shana, to be with women who were your intellectual inferiors."

The combination of the two-day hangover, my murdered wife and now my best partner telling me I had superiority issues, made me want ram my now clenched fist up his black ass. Just as I pulled back to crack his jaw, though, I stopped in mid stride. I took one look at my fist and wanted to crawl into a cave to safety, security and seclusion. Instead, I just walked over to Ramsey, looked at him with sorrowful eyes and gave him a hug. "Sorry, man."

"You know if you would've hit me, I was gonna have to put you down?"

I looked at him and laughed. Ramsey joined and I think we laughed so loud that the statue of Henry Grady heard us. Sometimes life dealt blows that were too painful to cry about, but today I felt as though I had to laugh to keep myself from crying.

"I'll go to AIU and look on the bulletin board for a used AMC. But I gotta' tell you, it may cost some duckies." He rubbed his fingers together. "Maybe a grand."

"I haven't heard that word duckies in a while," I said, rubbing my fingers together. "I got the money, don't you worry about that."

I reached in my pocket, peeled off ten one-hundred-dollar bills and handed it to him as he walked out the door. I was still carrying around some of the donation money the fellows at the department collected for me. The removal of economic insecurity was a strange feeling. Not that I was a poor man, but to hand over one thousand dollars without blinking an eye was as foreign to me as eating spinach quiche.

I sat at my desk staring at the blank monitor. I had nothing else to do, so I pressed play and continued watching one of the surveillance tapes from Emory University Hospital.

Emory was founded at Oxford by the Methodist Church in 1836 and had nine major academic disciplines. Originally it was the Atlanta College of Physicians specializing in nursing and medical studies. Now, the world-renowned institution concentrated on cardiac care, organ transplants and neurosurgery. I didn't see any neurosurgeons enter through the main entrance. They probably parked their S class Mercedes in elaborate parking decks with glassed encased tunnels that led to private entrances. What I did see were everyday people, some looking rushed and worried while others dressed in their business-as-usual expression.

As the taped rolled, I eventually saw one doctor wearing a white lab jacket with a shirt and tie enter through the main entrance. He was an average-sized man with thick black hair. Then I saw Shana enter through the sliding glass door. My heart stopped at the site of her. She looked hurried, but she smiled as she stopped to speak to the information clerk. From what I could detect, the two women knew each other more personally than passing acquaintances. It was tricky focusing on that quadrant when the other three were a constant distraction.

Shana started at as an intern at Emory right after completing her dissertation. Most intern programs in psychology offer med students the opportunity the experience action in mental health, education or research. Shana chose mental health because she wanted to be a one-woman crusade to save people from dependence, nervosa and disorders that rob them the lifestyles she thought they deserved. She received a modest stipend for the three years of her residency and after fulfilling her licensing duties stayed at Emory to care for her growing client base. Where the clients paid Shana's attending psychologists, after her residency, she collected all the fees, paid rent to the University for her offices, and hired a secretary to field calls and file insurance paperwork.

Then Shana left the camera's field of vision. I searched for a pen and pad to jot the time of her first sighting. I purchased over two thousand dollars worth of office supplies and neglected to get the basics – paper and pencils. I stopped the tape and rushed out of the building, looking for a drug store.

I found a small non-franchised store on the corner that had one of those old-fashioned pharmacies from the fifties. I purchased a few items, including notebooks, pens, pencils, post-it notes, a corkboard, a white board and pushpins.

When I returned to the office, I played the tape and watched it until Ramsey walked in with a box in hand.

The Avid Media Composer was a slate gray apparatus about the size of a BETA machine, but with more bells and whistles. It had two VHS bays with as many slots for digitally enhanced media storage. We spent the rest of the day configuring the AMC for the inverse feed modulation, then finally figured out how to connect the serial interface of the AMC to one of the I/O ports on my computer and run the quickstart application at the command line interface. Ramsey had been afraid he wouldn't remember any of the technical configurations, but by dinnertime he got a menu to pop on screen leading us to the inverse feed. We were rocking and rolling. I picked one of the tapes, labeled it as 'Tape 1' and inserted it in the AMC. I pulled out one of the notepads and labeled it as such. Ramsey performed the task on the instructions to isolate the feed and when we saw the single feed we let out a big *Yeah!*

I looked at Ramsey and he let out a yawn.

"Hey man, why don't you go home and get some sleep?" I asked.

"Naw, I'm here for you, man," he said, trying to blink moisture into his reddening eyes.

"I'm just gonna sit here and look through these four tapes that we edited, then I'm going home. Get out of here and get some sleep."

Ramsey left and I felt lucky to have such a good friend that was willing to sacrifice his day off to help me. When I heard the outer door close, I got up to lock it. Night had fallen and the clear skies offered a peaceful view of lights of the Atlanta skyline dancing with the stars. I realized that I hadn't eaten since breakfast, so I called information and got the number for Mandarin Gardens downstairs. I could've saved the ninety-five cents BellSouth charged and walked down one flight of stairs, but I figured that it would add to Aisha's bonus at the end of the year. I ordered the chicken and broccoli with two egg rolls and a Coke. Yun, the same guy who made us buy a meal in order to sit at one of the two tables, delivered my food. When I called, he informed me that he had a key to the door just for the purpose of delivery to the building's tenants.

As I sat at the desk and ate, I watched one of the tapes we converted. It was the emergency room surveillance area. I guessed when they built hospitals, they had in mind to make all of them uniform. The emergency room at Emory looked like any other emergency room I'd ever been in. They had that beige commercial grade vinyl tile with cinder-blocked hallways. There was a nurse's station in the middle of the room surrounded by about ten semi-private patient rooms with glass windows and doors.

I watched the entire day in the emergency room and nothing stood out as odd. I put the second tape in and began watching. It was a major corridor of three hallways merging together. I saw so many people that it was hard for me to focus. I slowly dozed off, the takeout carton in my lap.

I woke out of my languorous slumber to a scratching noise outside the door. I listened carefully in the direction of the hallway and heard it again. I slowly rose from my chair and headed to the door. I took care to keep my shadow from showing on the other side of the privacy glass. When I leaned forward to get an earshot of the noise, the door to my office opened with a loud *thud.* At that instant, I went rigid, paralyzed as a vagrant stepped into my office.

My fire department training on self-defense kicked in. When I tapped the burglar on the shoulders, he turned quickly in a startled motion and I tactically struck his right lung cavity area with the butt of my palm. The department taught me that this strategic thrust of the palm yields the maximum results to knock a man off his feet. In this case, not only did I knock him off his feet, but I must've also knocked the wind out of him. He stooped over his bent knee, gasping for air.

I grabbed the unkempt man and dragged him down the stairs by the back of his collar.

"If I catch you or any of you family members in this building again, I'll do more than knock the wind out of you."

When I released him, he ran off into the night and disappeared.

I walked upstairs a bit leery about the empty building. All my senses were on a heightened state of alert as I checked the lock to see how the burglar got in. No damage had been done because it was a simple lock to jimmy. I stood in the center of the room contemplating whether I should review more tapes or call it a night. The thought of Dana helped me to make up my mind. I wanted to be fresh and well rested for my visit.

I picked Dana and Chloe up and spent the morning at SciTrek, a private organization that housed workshops and exhibits exploring technologies that affect everyday life. SciTrek's interactive approach demystified science, math, and technology and made it exciting. Dana ate it up. Her favorite exhibit was the electricity and magnetism display that tickled the back of her neck.

As we headed for lunch at McDonald's, I peered in the review mirror and watched Dana and Chloe chatter about their plans for a birthday party. I felt that familiar pang of loneliness, knowing that her life was going on without me.

During lunch, Dana let me know that she needed an outfit to go with the purse I purchased from one of the vendors on Marietta Street. I felt a wave of relief at her normalcy, in spite of her mother's death. After I spent too much money at the Gap Kids store, she was anxious to get back to Aisha's and get dressed for the party.

When I dropped her off, Aisha was putting on a fresh pot of coffee. Not that any of her coffee sat around long enough to get muddy. I sat at the kitchen table and drank a cup. I wrote her a sizable check for Dana's everyday incidentals.

Aisha looked at the check. "Rick, you know you don't have to do this?"

"And you don't have to look after Dana while I–"

"While you what?" she asked, concerned.

"Never mind," I said, trying to figure out why I opened my mouth. Probably just to change feet.

"Rick Edison, what are you up to?" She stared at me.

When a woman, whether she's your mother or not, calls you by both names, it generally implies that she means business. I shrugged and told her about the surveillance tapes and my hopes to find Shana's killer.

She paused and lit a cigarette. "And if you find him, what are you going to do? Tap him on the shoulders and tell him that you are making a citizen's arrest?"

"I'm thinking more on the lines of strangling him."

"That's my point. You just spent a day with Dana. If she loses her father, then what?"

"Don't worry about that, I won't kill him."

"What about if he kills you."

I pursed my lips. "Now you know that's not going to happen."

"He's killed before, remember?"

I thought about what she said but shrugged it off. I finished my coffee, gave her a hug, kissed Dana and left for my makeshift office.

I took the interstate and navigated my way to Alabama Street. When I passed Underground Atlanta, I marveled at the history of the institution. In the mid-eighteen-hundreds, the old downtown was defined by the Georgia Railroad Depot. To allow for safe and continuous street access over the railways, a system of bridges and viaducts were constructed above the old streets surrounding the rail depot. With overpasses one story above the street, the second story in effect became the first floor and the original street level was underneath, hence the birth of Underground Atlanta. In the sixties this underground city became a popular area filled with bars and clubs. Today it consisted of boutiques, restaurants and nightclubs.

Downtown Atlanta was pleasant on Saturdays, with only the new inner-city dwellers making their way to and from weekend errands. I was able to park right in front of Doc Jones' building and I looked around the glass canyon that once housed Atlanta's financial district. Now the city's financial hub was Peachtree Street. As I walked to the door, I saw a broken crack pipe on the ground, and understood why Doc swept the sidewalk in front of his building every morning.

I went straight to the AMC and converted the rest of the tapes. It was a good thing Ramsey thought to buy extra VHS tapes, because there were a total of twenty-four tapes to sift through. It was a harrowing ordeal. Before I got started, I numbered each tape before I viewed it and took notes in an organized fashion. The note-taking kept me from dozing off.

The hospital was a maze of corridors connecting to other corridors, branching off to more connecting corridors. Plus, for every corridor, there was a bank of elevators, every one with a different letter signifying that wing. I pulled off a separate sheet of paper and tried to create a blueprint of the hospital's floor plan. There were zillions of rooms – a mechanical room, fire control room, a gross room, whatever that meant, a mailroom, a print room and an oxygen storage room.... With so many hallways and rooms, I managed to see that the surveillance cameras were housed in a dome-shaped, mirrored encasement that served two purposes, to monitor the hallway and to act as a mirror for oncoming people traffic. I witnessed where a nurse avoided a collision with an elderly lady who concentrated her efforts on simply walking.

Instead of an ordinary wheelchair for patient transport, Emory had those fancy caddies that resembled a golf cart without the steel-supported top assembly. I watched and took notes as masses of people walked the hallways, until I saw Shana. The time stamp showed 7:43 p.m. I referenced it back to the first note I took of her arriving at the hospital, 7:28 p.m. By my calculations, it took her fifteen minutes to get to the neuroscience ward of Emory.

The ward sported blue vinyl tile and aqua walls that were more serene than the bland beige of other departments. I noticed that even the uniforms of the nursing staff were coordinated with the décor. I followed the sight of Shana until she turned down a corridor directly past the nurse's station and I lost sight of her. I immediately stopped the tape, ejected it and put another in its place. While the tape whirred, I wrote down the time that I lost sight of her, 7:44 p.m.

When the tape began, I fast-forwarded it to 7:40 and when I didn't see the familiar blue colors of the neuroscience ward, I stopped it and put in another tape. This cycle occurred through four additional tapes until I picked her back up on the fifth tape, turning a corner at 7:44 pm. My heart raced, I was certain of her destiny, just unsure of the time. I leaned back, looked over my shoulders and saw that the sun had set behind one of the skyscrapers.

When I cut my glance back at the screen, I saw a shadow of a man peeping around the corner, a few yards in front of Shana. I paused the AMC, got up and paced back and forth. My heart felt like it was beating against heavy metal. My hands were shaking so badly that I felt like I was in a detox program and even though I stopped smoking cigarettes years ago, I craved one badly.

For the first time in my adult life, I felt alone and scared. The room felt eerie, and I realized I was still jittery about last night's break-in. I reached over to rewind the tape, pressed play and the images on the silent screen came to life again. I must have rewound it farther than the 7:44 time because the monitor showed 7:38. I let it play. I noticed the back of the same doctor I saw entering the main area right before Shana entered. Since I had numbered and cataloged the tapes I knew which one it was and I grabbed it.

"I saw this dude once," I said out loud.

I looked at my notes and saw the time that I clocked Shana entering and fast-forwarded it to that time. What I saw only confirmed my earlier suspicion. I *thought* I saw a doctor come in the hospital's main entrance because of the white lab jacket. What I saw was a man bowing his head as he passed the camera. I replayed the tape, this time looking beyond the entrance. Nothing but a concrete wall behind the valet desk. Funny how I didn't notice the valet before. I rewound it again, this time watching for the direction he came from. When I saw that he entered from the left of the screen, I wrote a note as to that affect. Another oddity I noticed was his hair. I paused the tape with the man's picture frozen on the frame. Further examination revealed his knowledge of the camera. He knew what side to enter the door that would be less revealing. And I knew he was the man who murdered my wife.

8

I put in my twenty-four-hour shift the next day without leading Ramsey on about the discovery the night before. I didn't want the likes of JT, the web guru, getting a whiff of what I was doing. One time he disguised Cap's tragedy as a joke and circled it on the web like an African virus. After Cap's wife left him for a police officer, he e-mailed a joke that started as an officer chasing a man in a red corvette, just like Cap had. The joke continued with the officer telling the driver that he'd let him off with a warning if he could come up with a good excuse for speeding. The man informed the officer that his wife had left him for a policeman and that he was speeding in fear that the officer was trying to give her back. The officer told the man to enjoy the rest of his evening. Since then, I have been walking on thin ice when discussing personal matters around the station even though JT stopped with the jokes on account of his own wife divorcing him.

After our shift ended the next morning, I asked Ramsey to meet me at the office. We snaked in and out of traffic, with him stopping off for a couple of breakfast platters at McDonald's. I felt gritty wearing the same clothes since yesterday, but I was anxious for Ramsey to see the tape.

"I think I saw the guy who murdered Shana."

Ramsey was just about to gobble his entire hash brown patty, but put it down. "Why didn't you tell me yesterday at the station?"

"You know how JT is. I didn't want it posted on the Internet."

"OK, right. Let's take a look."

I hesitated.

"What's the problem, man?"

I shrugged. "I don't know. What if it's him? How do we find him and when and if we find him, what do we do?"

"Rick, I don't know, but I do know that if you want me to make him so unrecognizable that they have to swab him for DNA, then I'll do it."

"Now that part I can handle. I'm talking about the legal route. How would I get him to turn himself in after I beat the living shit out of him?" I asked, thinking about Aisha's concerns.

"Let's take a look." He nodded towards the AMC.

I reached over, inserted the tape and rewound it a few threads. As the silent images came to life I noticed it went back too far, but I let it play so I could take in a few more bites. Then we saw the same doctor enter the main entrance shortly before Shana. I froze the image for him to see.

"That's him."

"Rewind that again."

I did and watched as Ramsey studied the image.

"Damn, homeboy's trying to hide from us." Ramsey put his food down and ignored it. It was hard for me to continue eating as well.

"What color is his hair?" I asked.

He looked at me as if I slapped his mother. "It's black, Sherlock, very black."

"Yes, it is very black and very thick, too."

Ramsey looked at his hair again as I replayed it for him.

"It's a wig," he said.

I found the spot and paused the tape so that the man's picture was frozen on the screen. He knew the location of the camera. He knew what side to enter the door that would be less revealing. And he wore a wig. I looked at Ramsey.

"He knows this hospital."

"But how?" Ramsey asked, staring at the monitor.

"Maybe he works there."

"Or maybe he *used* to work there."

"I wonder if Director Leggett would be willing to give us a list of fired employees?"

Ramsey leaned forward. "You're pushing your luck."

"I love you too, Ramses."

"So it shall be written, so it shall be done."

It never failed, every time I called him Ramses from *Moses*, he came back with the same line.

It turned out to be one of those beautiful Atlanta mornings with the sky looking like a Hollywood scene. As I gazed out of the window, I wondered what I was doing. I didn't have the resources that I needed to find out the identity of the wigged man. Only the Atlanta Police Department had the authority and the resources needed to advance with the lead, and those bobble-heads probably couldn't put M&M's in alphabetical order. I needed their help and I didn't like it, at all.

I looked at Ramsey.

"I guess I need to take this tape to the police."

"An impasse?"

"You've been reading again, haven't you?" I smiled at Ramsey and grabbed the two tapes of the mystery man, and we left.

We took the Expedition since it was parked closer than his truck. I intended to show Leicky and Biddings the tape in hopes that we could work together, plus I thought this new evidence would exonerate me as a suspect. When I turned onto Ponce from Glen Iris, there was a full-blown media event happening at the precinct. The local news networks each had their satellite uplink trucks positioned in front of the building with reporters and cameramen swarming the front entrance like it was the OJ trial redux. I had been so engrossed in finding Shana's murderer that I was totally zoned out from the city's current events.

We tried in vain to find a parking spot in the main parking garage, the same one Leicky and Bidding drove me into to identify Shana's body. I had to swallow hard in order to push down the vile that threatened to boil up. We had to exit the garage and park at the Cactus car wash across the street.

When we walked to the main lobby, we were barraged with reporters asking if we knew the child molester. From what we learned, a physical education teacher had been caught molesting a twelve-year-old *girl.* I could see the headlines, 'Lesbian coach fondles girl.'

That was my first time inside the lobby of the East Precinct and it smelled like the dusty old building that it was. Sears and Roebuck housed their catalog division there during fifties. I envisioned women sitting at their desk with those tight skirts, fuzzy angora sweaters and narrow pumps, answering the black rotary dial telephones. I felt like I stepped back in time just being in that building.

When we reached the front desk, I saw an overweight sergeant manning the desk. He wore a white uniform shirt with the sewn-in pleats, a gun in a shoulder holster and a big beer belly. He wore one of those stainless steel name badges, that read Amos.

"I want to talk to Detective Leicky."

"Name?" Sergeant Amos asked, not bothering to look up.

"His name is Detective Leicky." I couldn't help letting that slip out.

"I don't have time for any bullshit–"

"Rick Edison."

He looked at me and yanked the phone from the receiver. Evidently Sears left the same black rotary dial phones in the building because that's exactly what he used. He stared at the ceiling as he waited for Leicky to answer.

"He's not in. You want to leave a message?"

I hadn't thought of a plan B, but instead I asked him for Biddings and when he called another number, Biddings picked up. After a few moments on the phone, the desk jockey told me to grab a seat and Biddings would be down.

I sat on a bench and waited fifteen minutes. The crowd of people was incredible. Not only was there a parade of reported vying for the best spot to tape commentaries, there was also the people of Atlanta either being processed, visiting loved ones in the city lockup or making reports on missing persons. Most people neither looked my way nor did they give me a second thought when they did look at me. I wondered what it would be like to work in such a gloomy atmosphere. Then I saw her.

Kimisha walked in and strutted to the desk sergeant. When I saw him shaking his head, I knew she failed to get the scoop she'd come for. When she turned to leave, she spotted us sitting on the bench.

"You want to tell me why you're here?"

"I'd rather not." As soon as I said it I regretted the words leaving my mouth. She had done nothing but try to help me and I returned the favor with a smart-assed remark.

"Rick, let me try to make something clear. I put my name and reputation on the line for you so you could get those surveillance tapes and now, you're here at the police station." She hesitated. "I want to make sure the cops won't be coming after me today or tomorrow."

"Kimi, I don't think you have to worry about that. It's me they want."

I explained to her how I punched Leicky in the jaw the first day I met him. I told her that he warned me to keep my nose out of his investigation and I then reminded her of my arrest. She took all this in.

"You have a set of steel balls, don't you?"

I had a range of mixed emotions when I heard her say that to me. After having explained that I assaulted an officer, it made me feel stupid that she was condescending, but on the other hand it turned me on to hear a woman of her caliber refer to me as a man with steel balls. I shook off the second feeling as quickly as it fostered. "More like balls of stupidity."

"I was going to say that but I didn't want to sound condescending."

I cocked my head sideways, wondering if I was I thinking out loud. "Thank you for being gentle."

I remained silent, not knowing what to say next.

"There's one piece of the puzzle missing. Why are you here?"

I had no problem talking about the mystery man I saw lurking around the corner in the neuroscience ward. I explained that I wanted the police to use their resources to extrapolate the image and run it against known criminals. She let out a cute little smirk.

"You are becoming quite a sleuth, aren't you?" She didn't wait for an answer and I didn't offer one. "Did the detectives look at the tapes?"

Then Biddings walked over to us. I stole a look at my watch and realized forty minutes had gone by since I first came in. I glared in the direction of the desk sergeant.

I stood up. "Detective Biddings, I have a tape of the night Shana was murdered. There's a suspicious-looking man following her around the hospital." I glanced at Ramsey and Kimi for quiet support.

"Sorry, we can't help you." His eyes hardened. "Seems we have a missing file on your wife's case."

The heat from my body rose and I wanted to let it out, on his face. "How do you lose a file on a murder of a prominent doctor?"

"You tell me." He gave me a strong look.

"You think I took it, right?" I threw my hands up in disgust. My voice grew louder. "Why don't you blame me for everything. Hell, don't stop now, blame me for the kid's molestation while we're all here."

When I said those words, I felt a hush come over the lobby of the precinct like some kind of scene in a horror movie. And then the reporters rushed our way. Kimi grabbed my hand and led me away from the oncoming herd.

"Put your head down," she whispered as she whisked me out of the precinct through the side entrance. I felt an adrenaline rush as I have never been accosted by a swarm of reporters. We got in her car and sped off as camera crews filmed our escape. I let out an exasperated sigh.

"What the hell was that all about?" Kimi asked when we reached a safe distance away.

"I have no–"

"We have the file," Ramsey said from the backseat.

Kimi slammed on the brakes and momentarily lost control of the vehicle. When we came to a safe stop, Kimi and I turned to the back seat and looked at Ramsey.

"What?"

Ramsey looked at me with questioning eyes and glanced at her.

"What is it, Ramsey, she's just as much a part of this as we are."

"The day we went to see Leggett. I swiped the file from the car, remember?"

"What are you guys talking about here?"

I ignored her question. "Why didn't you tell me you had Shana's file?"

"Man Leggett had me so stupefied, I forgot all about it." He looked away like he did something bad. "The file is still under my truck seat."

"Damn, we've been sitting on the file all this time." I turned back around and bit my knuckles until they turned pink.

Kimi looked at me with accepting eyes and I wanted to hug her to make all of this go away. I wanted to lose myself in her beauty and her body. I rationalized that it was my libido talking and focused on the problem.

"Do we give it back to them?" I asked.

"Hell no." Kimi jumped in. "We go somewhere and look it over, now!"

And with that we made it to the office. I still had the tape in my hand, but I put it aside as Ramsey sat the file on the desk. We looked at it first like it was a decapitated body part, no one willing to make the first move. Then Kimi, sitting on the couch, got up and removed the file. She returned to the couch and looked through it, slowly. Ramsey moved to her side. I gnawed on my knuckles again and when I bit down too hard, I changed hands. The agony I saw on her face when she flinched made me question my motives for viewing the contents. I got up and walked to the door, then to the window, all the while chompping on my hand. When I felt something warm and sticky, I looked down to see that I had broken the flesh and blood trickled out. Sucking the blood from the abrasion, I sat down next to her.

"You sure you want to see this?"

"Uh – yeah, I have to." I forced myself to focus on the murderer and not my emotions. "I can't come this far and turn away."

I sat next to Kimi. The file contained a lot of forms, documents with serial type numbers on them. Each form had typed information and sections for comments that were either handwritten or typed. Just glancing at some of the pages, without critical study, I saw my name a couple of times. When Kimi flipped to the next page, the contents of my stomach erupted in such a forceful way that I had to dash to the wastebasket and throw up. I heaved convulsions that felt like I jarred a few organs from their socket.

Shana's body was contorted in a mangled position in a biohazard Dumpster. Her body lay on red bags with the hazard symbols on them. Hypodermic needles busted out of the bags and pierced her body as it impacted with the trash. Her blouse was ripped and the crotch area of her pants was torn out. I marshalled the courage to see the entire file. The crime scene unit took pictures of every angle possible. And when I saw the close-up of her eyes, I felt traumatized. The eyes looked like one of those Michael Angel statues with the vacant, disembodied stare. The sclera were ripped apart and I couldn't tell that they were once white.

"I'm gonna find the sick son of a bitch who did this to my wife and rip his eyes out with my bare hands." Then I let out a primordial scream, looking to heaven, questioningly.

Kimi put the file aside, got up and held me tight. She clutched my body so long that I envisioned being cocooned in a better existence than this evil place we call earth.

"Let's watch the tapes so we can find him," she said when she released me.

I stumbled, trying to put the tape in the AMC, and fumbled with the remote control. Kimi sat there and smiled at me, all the while remaining silent. She was so cool. Ramsey's attentions were still on the file. When I finally got the image of the mystery man to appear on the screen, I paused it.

"There he is," I said rather loudly with clenched fists.

Kimi leaned closer to the TV monitor and I caught a whiff of her perfume. I was totally unfazed by it. She studied the figure with astute concentration. I admired her strong will and determination.

"Rick, I have to tell you, this may be more difficult than I imagined." She pointed to the man's face. "You see here, there are no visible facial characteristics showing."

Ramsey looked up and when I viewed it with the mindset of facial characteristics, I had to agree with her. There were no visible traits. In fact, at closer glance I really couldn't determine if the image was a man or woman. I rested my elbows on my knees and buried my head in the palm of my hands in total despair. "Well, thanks for taking a look," I mumbled.

"Don't go getting dopey on me now," she said as her expression changed from gloom to optimistic. "Let me have a copy of the tape and I'll call in a favor with a tech over at CNN."

I lifted my head up with a new sense of anticipation. "A tech at CNN?"

"Yeah, those guys have all the techno-gadgets that can transcode a video format to a high-quality image."

"Is that right? How do you know all of this?"

"Let's just say that the first rule for becoming a reporter is to have a natural curiosity for everything," she said, letting out a smile. "Plus, we have a machine that can take an image from a video feed. I can run it against our database of known criminals. Maybe we can get a match with the silhouette."

My spirits lifted as she said this. Finally someone with the means to help and the brains to do it. "Thank you very much."

The gravity of the situation was momentarily lifted.

I quickly jumped up and made a copy of the mystery man's two images. I had to input a few commands in my PC to execute the task.

Kimi looked at me with a grin on her face. "You're getting good with your own techno-gadget."

Kimi left with the copy and I decided to look at the other tapes. After seeing the grisly pictures, my determination to find him incrusted my whole being. I watched several grueling hours of people coming and going and it gave me a headache, but as I rubbed my temples, something dawned on me. I had not seen Shana leave.

I went to my notes and looked up the tape where I saw her enter the neuroscience ward. I found it and put it in the AMC. When I finished the tape, I rewound it and watched it again. Both times I saw Shana enter the patient room, but neither time did I see her leave.

Her body was thrown in the Dumpster at Emory, so I assumed she was murdered in the hospital. But how did she leave the room? My head pounded as I tried to think of something, anything logical. It just didn't add up.

As I tried to ward off my headache, the telephone rang and scared the shit out of me. I believe that's the first time the phone ever rang and that reminded me to call BellSouth to get the line disconnected. I answered on the third ring.

"Hello."

There was no answer.

"Hello." Then I heard a soft click followed by a dial tone.

I replaced the receiver and thought little more about it. I stared out the window and got back to my dilemma. How did her body get from the room to the Dumpster? Then a thought came to me. From what I could ascertain, Emory had the surveillance cameras every fifty feet or so, and if I looked, maybe I could find another camera down a connecting corridor to the neuroscience ward.

I replayed the tape in the fast-forward mode, looking for a surveillance camera hidden in the mirrored dome. As I studied the images, I realized that I was seeing only one angle. But then I saw a nurse walking to a corridor, down the hall from the room Shana entered. She looked up as I had seen so many employees do. I assumed she was looking at the overhead dome mirror to prevent a collision with an oncoming person. I quickly popped the tape out and put another one in, hoping to find that camera. I made a mental note to look for the aqua walls.

Two tapes later, I found the neuroscience ward. I looked at my notes for the time I saw Shana enter the patient room. Then I fast-forwarded the tape to precisely ten minutes before her sighting. When I played it back, people passed the intersection and others turned the corner. Then I saw the mystery man, only he had his head down.

"Dammit."

My lips curled in disgust as he waded out of view. The tape kept rolling for twenty-some minutes when I saw Shana. She actually turned the corner and walked directly toward the camera. I jumped up and quickly stopped the tape.

She stood there, frozen in time. She was so beautiful and so alive at that moment. Had she known her fate? I wondered. I sighed in relief when I saw that she was safe, then it hit me that she wasn't safe, she was about to be murdered. I felt that familiar trapdoor open in the pit of my stomach. I started the tape and when I saw her turn left to the open stairwell, I caught myself shouting, *"Don't take the stairs!"*

I stared blankly at the monitor, realizing that she probably was mutilated in the stairwell where Emory had no cameras. The hopeless feeling that engulfed me at that moment felt like some satanic spirit sucking all the air out of me. In my agony, I hastily swiped my hand across the desk and flung the rest of the tapes on the floor, some hitting the wall. I was hungry, lonely, angry and tired. The four walls were not only closing in on me, they were collapsing. I had to get away.

I left the office and sped all the way to Aisha's house. I needed the comfort of Dana and her innocence to get me through the rage that threatened to take over. Dana greeted me with a big, jumping hug as I entered the house. Aisha beamed an expression of delight when she saw Dana's smile as I walked in.

She brought me a cup of coffee as I sat on the floor and listened to Dana tell me about the birthday party. I let myself get wrapped up in her life so I could forget about mine. She insisted on reading one of her beloved Dr. Suess books. And for the first time that I could remember, I agreed. We watched reruns of *Family Matters*, read some more and ate beef ravioli for dinner. She grabbed my face, pulled it to hers and gave me the biggest kiss. It was the most real thing in my life. I had to muster all the strength that my six-two body could find to hold back the bittersweet tears that welled up inside me. Aisha must have noticed because she saved me from having to explain myself.

"Come on, Dana, time for you and Chloe to go to bed."

"Oh, can I stay up a little longer?" Dana cooed.

I looked up at Aisha like I was a child asking for permission.

"OK, if you go take your bath, I'll let you stay up for a little while longer."

With that, Dana took off running. Aisha pointed her finger at me and directed me to the kitchen. She sat at the table and lit a cigarette. "What's going on with you, Rick?"

"Is it that obvious?" I grabbed one of her cigarettes.

"Put it this way, if I hadn't distracted you, I would've had to call the insurance company for that flood of tears."

"I saw Shana's killer."

Aisha bucked her eyes, "You what? What did you say to him? How did you find–"

"Hold on to your seat. I saw what looked like a suspicious man following her at the hospital. But I couldn't get a good enough view to match his face."

"What are you gonna do now?"

"I have someone looking at the tape trying to isolate the image."

"That sounds like a good start."

"Only thing is, the person on the video isn't showing any visible characteristics. We don't even know if it's a male or female because they seemed to know every camera angle at Emory."

"They have all kinds of new technology that can do all kinds of things with video images. I once saw on the Discovery Channel that somebody found a skull and a forensics sculptor produced a replica to a person with flesh-colored clay. They showed the picture on some show and somebody recognized the person."

"That's all well and good, but all I have is a picture, and that's wishful thinking."

"I also saw on the Discovery Channel that they could make a three-dimensional replica of a skull from a partial."

I looked at her in amazement. I hadn't thought of a life-like sculpture based on a picture. "You and that Discovery Channel. I would hate it if BellSouth found out that you were working from home watching TV."

"Better than those mind-numbing soap operas." She took one last puff of her cigarette and put it out.

Dana must have taken one of those sailor showers because she was back out in less time than it took for Aisha and I to smoke a cigarette.

We read some more and watched more television. I must have fallen asleep on the family room couch because when I woke up, Dana was cradled in the nook of my armpit. I had a cramp in my neck the size of a golf ball. A few hours later, I tiptoed around and gathered my things.

9

When I arrived at the station, I asked Spoon if he'd been taking pictures of Doc's building for some kind of promotion.

"Man, with all the referrals homey is giving me, I don't need to solicit for new business. The way I see it, I may be able to leave the fire department in a couple of years, if I play my cards right and stay sober one day at a time."

I never thought I'd see the day when Mathew Witherspoon looked to the future. Ramsey walked in, made his way over to the skillet that Spoon was cooking in, reached in and grabbed some eggs with his hands.

"Just help yourself, big boy," Spoon said, half-joking with Ramsey, who was nearly twice his size.

"You want some of this," Ramsey came back with.

"I'd whoop your ass with my eyes closed."

"You'd better think again."

I couldn't help but to break in. "Can we all just get along?"

Ramsey looked at me, then at Spoon. "I can't believe you said that lame ass phrase."

"It worked for Rodney," I said and walked out of the kitchen. I went to the day room and when I saw that no one was in there, I turned to the Discovery Channel.

I spent the day watching TV, catching up on my sleep and talking to Ramsey about the file. We talked in hushed tones.

"I can't decipher all the acronyms to piecemeal it together," Ramsey said softly.

"What do you mean?" I asked.

He looked around, insuring that no one was in the kitchen. "They performed a LD50 test for fifty-percent kill." He shrugged. "I don't have the first clue what that means."

"Neither do I."

"There's more. A TDLo test was performed and whatever it was, it gave a low dosage."

"Maybe the police report is a dead end, Ramsey. I mean if the police couldn't find a suspect other than me, then the chances of us finding something are slim to none."

"We tried." Ramsey got up and headed to the kitchen.

Shortly after, I heard a pounding noise coming from the kitchen counter, I heard Ramsey saying, "That's it."

I got up and headed toward the kitchen, bumping into Ramsey at the entryway.

"What is it?" I asked, expecting that he found a missing link.

"Do you remember…." he started, then did another quick room scan. Someone was lurking in the engine room and he led me outside.

"Remember when you, how should I say it, when you banged that girl who worked for the CDC?"

I tilted my head, trying to remember. I've been with a lot a women, it was hard to think of just one.

"Come on, Rick, you don't remember the women you slept with?"

I lowered my head, avoiding eye contact with him. This was a new feeling. Prior to Shana's murder, I had no problem boasting to Ramsey about my conquests, but today I felt embarrassed and ashamed for using women for my own selfish, co-dependant motives. "No."

"You told me that you stopped seeing her when you found out she worked around those viruses." He paced, trying to remember something. "What was her name?"

"I think it was Lily." It was coming back to me. We met at a softball game. The guys at the twenty-third were playing the men at the second. She started talking to me about my swing and the same evening, I was in her bed.

"No, I don't think that's it."

"Lisa," I exclaimed, feeling proud that I remembered.

"Give her a call. See if she'll help you with the tox report."

"Easier said than done." I turned to leave. "I dumped her, remember."

I muddled through the rest of the day, wondering if I should look her up. My mind kept swinging back and forth on whether to pay Lisa a visit. I settled on 'no' for the moment. I spent a few hours at the office the next day reading the police report, but I felt reluctant to look at the morbid pictures of Shana. I viewed a few of the tapes, hoping to pick up on something I missed. I began to get restless so, I wandered around the streets of downtown Atlanta.

I walked up Marietta Street until I reached Peachtree Street. I walked south on it until I reached the Flatiron building with its five ionic columns. I marveled at the angular structure that stood on a triangle lot bounded by Peachtree, Poplar and Broad Streets that once dominated the skyline. I decided to walk across the street and take in the sights of Woodruff Park. An anonymous benefactor originally donated it in 1973 and today it offered the best view of downtown Atlanta, with a large, multi-tiered fountain that provided a good lunch respite for the nine-to-five hostages to relax among jazz and rock bands. As I sat on one of the many benches, my cell phone rang and I reached to grab it.

"Hello."

"Rick, this is Kimi. I have something for you. My connection at CNN did what he could with the tape and he wants to give it to you personally."

"That's cool. Just tell me when and where and I'm there."

We made plans to meet the next day at Centennial Olympic Park, which sat caddy-corner from the CNN Center.

I had a bounce in my step knowing that we got an ID on the bastard. With the high confidence I decided to pay a visit to the CDC.

The Center for Disease Control was surprisingly close to Emory. I wondered if Shana and Lisa had crossed paths, unaware they slept with the same man. I questioned how I would feel in the presence of a man Shana had slept with. Just thinking that, I felt a surge of jealousy spike my heart. When I made it to what appeared to be the main building, I saw a sign that said the CDC was an agency of the Public Health Service. The building looked like a four-story high school with all the windows. Why would they house so many infectious diseases in a building with so many opportunities for seepage?

When I approached the lobby, I asked the receptionist for Lisa Merriwether. While she called, I wrote down all my numbers for her, I had a feeling this was going to be a brief conversation. Lisa walked out to greet me a few moments later.

She wore a white lab jacket and her hair was pulled back in a ponytail. She gained a few pounds since I last saw her and wore a pair of rimless eyeglasses. I was timid about requesting a favor because of the pain that I caused her, but resolved to ask her anyway.

"How have you been?" I winced, expecting the hands-on-the-hip-neck-rolling-lashing out.

"Quite well," she offered, letting the silence linger in the air.

That wasn't too bad. I glanced around and saw the receptionist looking our way. "Can we go somewhere and talk?"

"Rick, I'm a married woman now. We don't have anything to say to each other."

How dare she get married on me? I thought to myself, somehow reasoning that my great lovemaking would keep women from seeking love from other men. I shook off my conceited thoughts, not sure where it came from. "No, it's nothing like that. I need your help with something."

I explained to her about the toxicology report, leaving out the method of acquisition, and asked if she'd take a look at it.

She thought about it for a second and came back with, "No. I will not jeopardize my career for you." Her hands went to her hips. "I can't believe you. You think you can waltz in here, after dumping me, and ask a favor?"

I no longer liked the word *dump.* "I'm sorry if I hurt you, Lisa. I didn't mean for you to get so involved with me."

"You are one arrogant asshole. I wasn't mad at you for hurting me. Hell, I just wanted sex and not a relationship like you thought." Her voice rose and she glanced around. She led the way to the door. "I'm refusing to help you because you didn't have the decency to tell me why you stopped seeing me."

"I'm sorry, I'm a changed man now." I handed her my numbers. "Please, just take it."

She looked at the piece of paper that I scribbled on and laughed at me as she walked away. "Good-bye, Rick."

I can't believe she laughed at me. No one ever laughed at me before. Something had changed with my charisma with women. I left as quickly as I had come. At least I gave the Lisa-angle a try. So what if I failed with her, I was soon going to have the face of the dastard.

When I arrived at the park the next day at noon, I looked around for Kimi. Centennial Olympic Park housed twenty or so acres of green space located virtually in the center of downtown. It was originally created for the 1996 Olympic Games, and now it was festive with plazas, memorials and a venue for concerts and weddings. The colorful commemorative bricks lined the walkways, surrounding a five-ring fountain that spewed jetting streams of water.

I caught sight of Kimi and another guy at the at the rendezvous point. Even from a distance, he looked scrawny with knock-knees. He wore khaki pants and a white short-sleeved shirt without an undershirt, and I had to hold back a look of disgust as I saw his nipples contrast his pale skin through his worn shirt. He wore a pair of outdated QG glasses that were trendy in the eighties. The only thing missing was a pocket protector, but then I saw two pagers attached to his belt, one of which looked like a two-way.

Kimi introduced him as Durden McDeevil.

I offered my hand. "I owe you a big thanks for helping me."

He shifted the brown paper sack lunch from one hand to the other and shook mine. "OK, fine."

His hands felt squishy and I had a mind to walk over to the fountains to rinse my hand off. I don't know if it was the clammy hands or his uptight position that made me think he wasn't much of a people person, but I do know that with a name like Durden McDeevil, he had some run-ins with the school kids. I was willing to bet that the kids ragged him by calling him 'Dirty Mac'.

"Were you able to capture any pictures?"

Dirty Mac looked at me irritably and sat down on the bench directly behind us. "It's not that simple." He crossed his legs like one of those modish ladies and looked at me through those glasses that made his eyes look larger.

"I'm willing to pay, if that's what you're talking about," I said and sat down on the bench opposite to him.

"Rick, I don't think he's talking about that," said Kimi.

"I can handle this, Kimisha," he said putting a sarcastic slant on the middle syllable, making it sound *Kimeeesha.*

"OK, I'll stay out of it." She walked a short distance away, not going out of earshot. I couldn't help wondering what kind of hold this geek had on Kimi. I know she said he owed her a favor but I couldn't imagine what it was. McDeevil broke my thought.

"I had to integrate the broadcast topology into real-time primary and secondary color correction. This gave me a video format that I could transcode into a seamless recompression."

He must have seen the mystified look of confusion on my face because he changed directions. But before he spoke, he picked at his cuticles with his incisors.

"Have you ever seen a movie where the computer monitor shows an emulation of a human made up of green lines?"

"Right, like Schwarzenegger in *The Sixth Day*?"

He stared blankly. "Yes like that. I used the Pinnacle Blue software architecture to edit the newly compressed format." He reached underneath his armpit to retrieve the file folder he carried. I hoped he wasn't expecting me to touch it.

"I took the compressed format and ran an isometric view decoder to come up with a shape of a head." He handed me glossy slide.

"A shape? What am I supposed to do with a shape of a head?" I was furious at McDeevil, the drip, for giving me the techno-garbo spiel, but no photo. I came to get a fleshed-out picture a man and not some isometric compressed bullshit. Everything was turning up a dead end.

I saw Kimi out of the corner of my eye. In one smooth swipe across her neck with her finger, she told me to cool it.

"Let me finish," he said in a don't-jump-to-conclusions tone. "From the top view of an isometric depiction, we produced a three-dimensional geometric computer model like this picture." He pointed to the glossy. "With reconstruction, a craniofacial replica can be produced with clay."

He paused and unwrapped his tuna fish sandwich and took a bite out of it. While he ate, I thought about Aisha's Discovery Channel program. I shook my head thinking about all the little bits of information and putting it together like a five-thousand-piece jigsaw puzzle. They couldn't pay me enough money to be a homicide detective like Leicky and Biddings.

"Let me see if I understand you," I said as McDeevil continued eating his lunch.

I noticed that Kimi had made her way back on the bench with us.

"You took a computer graphed view of the top of his, or her head and–"

"It's a man's head," he interrupted me. "That I know for sure, because the frontal eminence is larger in a male than a female. And this man's FE is huge." He let out an erratic laugh at his attempt to humor. I didn't get the joke.

I looked at the photo and had to agree with him. "So with this picture of a skull, I can go to Skulls 'R' Us and ask for a human-like replica?"

"I'm sorry if you find this funny," McDeevil said as he jammed the remainder of his lunch back in the brown paper sack and got up to leave. He turned to Kimi. "I refused to be talked down to."

Kimi jumped up and whispered something in his ear. After a few seconds, he looked over at me. He and Kimi spoke a few more hushed words and he gave her the file, then walked away. Kimi came back and sat down. I felt like a little kid who just got caught throwing a baseball through the neighbor's picture window. I didn't like the way I felt and I especially did not like the look she gave me.

"Rick, I know you are experiencing rage and anger about the murder of your wife," she began, slowly regaining her composure. "Durden was trying to help you and all you can do is offer snide remarks."

She looked away as the laughter of a toddler playing near the water fountain broke her thoughts. "Haven't you learned that you can get more with honey than with vinegar?"

"Jesus, Kimi, the guy's a geek."

"It's doesn't matter. You wanted something from him – maybe you should have tried to rein it in a little." She played with her fingernails and I noticed that they were not the acrylic ones from Lee Nails, or somewhere like that. "Just know that people are generally good-natured and want to help. If you approach them with respect."

"You might be right." I let out one of my better smiles.

"I know I'm right and no, that razzle-dazzle smile ain't gonna to help you." She got downright home-girl on me.

I need to double-check myself to make certain that I wasn't thinking out loud. Then something came to mind. "Kimi, why did you let him talk to you that way?"

She began biting her cuticle just like Durden had. "He's my brother."

"But he's white."

"We have different fathers. I don't know why I'm telling you this."

"So you're half white?"

"I prefer the term bi-racial."

I realized then, that she could have drilled me about my attitude towards her brother, but she let it slide, eliminating the subsequent defense mode.

After I left Centennial Olympic Park, I decided it was in my best interest to get into Leicky and Biddings' good graces, at least for now, so I headed for the East Precinct. Before I made my way there, I stopped by Kinko's on North Ave and made a few color copies of the skull.

I was becoming so familiar with the precinct, I felt as though I worked there. When I locked up the Expedition and walked towards the main lobby, I thought about Dr. Van Hart. She worked in the basement of the precinct. Maybe she knew something that could help. So instead of making my way to the street entrance of the mammoth building, I walked around to the morgue door. I pursed my lips, wondering how I was going to get in. I decided to ring the buzzer and try my luck, and in an instant later, the door buzzed open.

I saw the guard sitting at his desk when I walked in. I vaguely remembered seeing him the first time I came to the city morgue.

"I have some ID pictures for Dr. Van Hart," I said, giving my best effort at proper English, like I'd heard Ramsey do.

"Name?"

"Detective McDeevil," I lied.

He studied me for what seemed like a very long time. This whole experience of acting like I was someone else felt foreign. Why a morgue needed the likes of a guard, I did not know. He pushed a sign-in sheet across the desk. "Sign here."

When I walked down the corridor, I let out a sigh of relief. I looked around the drab walls and wondered why anybody in their right mind would choose a profession where their customer lacked social interaction skills. As I reached the stairwell, I inhaled the familiar reek of decomposing bodies hidden under the mist of Lysol spray.

I walked into Dr. Van Hart's office while she sat at a desk, head buried in a file. When I tapped on the doorframe she glanced up over her reading glasses with a look of surprise.

"Mr. Edison, what are you doing here?"

"I need you to check out my wrist, I think it's infected." This lying was getting easier.

Dr. Van Hart came around the desk, lifted my healthy wrist, examined it and looked up with a frown.

"That's not why you came here," she said as she dropped my wrist.

"You did a good job, considering–" I glanced down, wondering why I let those words slip out.

"Considering that I haven't worked on a on a living being in years."

Damn.

"I'm sorry. My mouth gets me in more trouble than I care to admit."

"What can I do for you?" She crossed her arms over her chest.

"I was wondering if I can take you to lunch and talk to you about something. I have something here," I said, holding out the photos of the skull that was in the file folder I carried in with me. "And please call me Rick."

She grabbed the entire folder, and took her time looking at the images Durden McDeevil produced. When she removed her reading glasses, I studied her smooth dark skin and admired her for the simplicity she exuded.

"Where did you get these from?"

"I really don't think I can tell you."

She handed the folder back to me. "Well, I really don't think I can help you."

Ouch, that hurt.

"OK," I said. "But can we go someplace more private?"

She gazed around the office candidly. "Doesn't get any more private than a morgue."

After we sat down, I explained how I got involved in the murder investigation. I told her about Leggett giving me the surveillance tapes, being careful to leave off the AJC stunt with Kimi. I explained the mystery man and his successful effort to avoid all the camera angles. Then I got to the part about Durden McDeevil and the computer-generated photo of the skull he created.

"So what is it that you want from me?" she asked with a critical squint.

"I was hoping that maybe you could make a three-dimensional replica from the picture."

She smiled at me suspiciously, "What do you know about 3-D replication?"

"No more than the Discovery Channel makes public."

"The Discovery Channel gives the layman enough information to make him dangerous," she said, raising her eyebrows at me.

"How so?"

"There is so much more to 3-D replication than that channel leads on." She paused and walked over to the skeleton frame that stood in the corner of her office. Pointing to the skull, "At precise anatomical points here and here, which are called T lines, there is an iterative point algorithm that can match crest lines, here, to attain global parametric transformation." She paused and placed her hands on her face while looking at the skeleton as if she was waiting for him to respond. "Of course, this technique can be accomplished by prescribed lengths of clay glued to the skull at precise anatomical points, which is called craniofacial identification."

"Can you do it?" I asked, not knowing what else to say.

"That is a good question. I am very interested to see if I can do it *without* a skull."

I shrugged my shoulders, I had no idea what she was talking about. She picked up the photos and fanned through them while keeping one eye on the skeleton, as if he was going to walk out.

"Listen very closely, Rick. I will consider helping you with this, only because I find it interesting." She pointed at me. "I want you to promise me that, if and only if I give you a recognizable face, you won't go ballistic on the guy like you did with my view window."

"OK, you have my word."

"No, I want you to promise me."

"Promise."

Before I left, I reached around her desk and grabbed a pink Post-It note and wrote down my cell, home and station numbers.

I left the basement and exited the metal doors, to speak with Leicky and Biddings next. Coming from the cool depths of the basement morgue, the hot afternoon humid air outside felt stifling. I picked up my pace. When I entered the front lobby and felt the air-conditioning, the beads of sweat that gathered on my back began to dissipate.

The sun filtered through the precinct windows revealing parallel motes of dust that stretched from one side of the lobby to the other. A different desk sergeant stood at the front counter. I walked over to one of the benches and pulled my cell phone off the belt clip. I called the number on the business card Leicky had given me. He answered on the second ring.

"Detective Leicky here."

"Detective, this is Rick Edison. I'm downstairs and I'd like to talk with you."

I heard laughter on the other end. "What's wrong, you want to spend another night in jail?"

"Very funny." I paused and considered my approach. "I owe you and Biddings an apology for my actions."

There was a pause and for a moment, I thought he had hung up on me.

"Leicky, you still there?"

"I'll tell the desk sergeant to let you up."

The desk sergeant gave me directions up to Homicide on the fourth floor. When I got to the elevator bank, I noticed that they were the old open-caged motorcars. I waited for what seemed like a long time and decided to take the stairs.

When I reached four, I stopped to catch my breath. I felt the effects of the cigarette I smoked at Aisha's. From what I can tell, the Atlanta Homicide consisted of twelve desks butted together in pairs. A printer, fax and a copier lined the wall, and a stained white coffeepot sat atop a file cabinet. Leicky's and Biddings' desks were butted together so that when they sat down, they were face to face. I've seen this in movies and wondered why the floor designers chose that particular space arrangement.

From my observation, there were six homicide teams for the entire city, a low ratio to the nearly four million people. When I walked past other detectives on my way to Leicky's desk, I felt all eyes on me. Just being there made me feel guilty for nothing. I sat next to Leicky's and Biddings' desks.

"Thanks for your time," I said, stumbling on my words.

Leicky gave me a long and searching look.

"I need to apologize for punching you, Leicky." I looked at directly at him as I apologized.

"What's with the change in attitude?" Leicky asked.

"Let's just say I had an epiphany," I said, thinking about attracting bees with honey.

"I'd say you have our file and now you don't know what to do with it," Leicky said, snidely.

"You dickheads need to make up your minds," I yelled and noticed the other detectives looking on. "One minute you arrest and the next you accuse me of stealing a damn file, only to come to you for help." I stood up and raised my hands. "Which is it gonna be?"

Maybe things can be had by vinegar, because judging by their expression after my venomous hell-raising, they acknowledged the disparity of their outlook.

Leicky looked down at his interlocked fingers. "What do you want us to do? We have a mad husband, a dead wife and a threatening tape." He looked at me quizzically. “All fingers pointed to you.”

“Only the judge didn’t think so at the arraignment.” I leaned over my lap. “Listen, man,” I said to Leicky, “I didn’t kill my wife. Check the phone records – I was trying to call her all night to apologize.”

Leicky cut a quick look at Biddings, at which point Biddings shrugged. “Get down to BellSouth right now and verify that.” Leicky ordered.

Biddings rose from his seat, pushing the chair back hard enough so it whacked the desk behind him.

“You’re letting him do it,” Biddings hissed before he walked out.

In one quick glance, Leicky cut him off before he was able to get in another snide remark. He sat up in his chair and straightened his jacket.

“Did you get tapes from Emory surveillance?” I asked.

“That was a dead end.”

It was ironic that I was able to get an outline of a skull and these lame pigeons were not doing anything with the lead. My rage threatened to flare up, but I remained calm.

“Can you take another look, maybe you missed a suspicious man dressing like a doctor, or something like that.”

“I can do that, but I ain’t promising nothing until Detective Biddings comes back with those phone records.”

“That’s fair.” I stood to leave when he spoke softly.

“We did find blood stains on the Dumpster that we think is the perpetrator’s.”

Then I sat back down and leaned closer. “What does that mean?”

“That means that when he threw your wife’s body over, he cut himself on a metal shard.”

“Did you come up with a match?”

“Unfortunately, he isn’t in the DNA database. No previous convictions, I’d say.”

“Figures.”

“One thing we do know, however, is that he has one helluva scar from the amount of blood he lost.”

10

I spent the rest of day waiting. I waited for Kimi's scan of the photo, I waited for Dr. Van Hart's craniofacial ID and I waited for something to happen. Nothing happened. The whole investigative process took too long and my patience wore thin. I had to do something.

I went to the office to view the tapes and while I was there I read the police file, again. Nothing. I even had the balls to go the Emory Hospital. My nerves were on end because I knew the cameras were tracking my every move. I kept going, knowing my innocence would prevail. I went up to the neuroscience ward, and decided to take the stairs to put myself where Shana was. The gripping feeling that swathed me while in the stairwell was so suffocating that I skipped steps to get to the ward faster.

Seeing the familiar aqua colors of the ward felt surreal, as I had watched it a dozen times on video. I walked to the patient room I witnessed her leaving and stood there. My hand went out to touch the door, wanting to feel her presence.

"Can I help you, sir?" a nurse said, scaring the shit out of me.

"I'm just – I'm here to see Durden McDeevil," I lied, using the same name that worked for me at the morgue, hoping that the surveillance team hadn't gone so far as to point one of those hyperbolic microphones at me.

"He's not in there. That room's empty." She walked to the nurse's station and I followed. "Spell the last name and I'll look it up." She typed in a command on one of the many computers and looked up at me.

I couldn't continue this lying – it felt too unnatural. Plus I didn't know how to spell the last name. *Why didn't I use Johnson?*

"I'm sorry, that's not why I'm here." I cut my glance away from her as she bore into me with blazing eyes.

"I don't have time for this. I'm calling security." She was a tough woman. I shouldn't have come but I had to make something happen. She lifted the receiver and punched in four digits.

Instinctively, I reached over the counter, pressed the button and cut off the dial tone. "I'm Rick Edison, my wife, Dr. Edison, was murdered here," I pleaded, releasing my finger from the phone.

She grabbed her mouth and took in a heavy gasp of air. “Oh my God, I’m so sorry.” She replaced the receiver and stood up. “I knew your wife. She was the kindest doctor in the hospital.”

Why didn’t I think to go the sympathetic route in the first place? “They haven’t found her killer and I needed to come here to see where she took her final breath.” I intended to use the sympathy ploy as long as I could.

“The way they tightened security around here, you’d think they were expecting him back.” She glanced around and leaned closer. “I heard that they’re even installing cameras in the stairwell.”

Too late now.

I got a look at her badge. “Sheila, I’m trying to find out who she was seeing the night she was murdered. Can you look that up for me?”

She pursed her lips and gave me a heavy look. “I can’t do that, sorry.”

“Can I call you and get it later?” I said as I nodded to one of the dome-shaped encasements that housed the camera. “I won’t tell a soul.”

“Sorry.”

I left Emory with nothing, just as I came. I went home and slept. I slept to forget, I slept to remember Shana, if only in my dreams.

I woke up grumpy and headed for work. I wanted to be alone – in my head renting space. I sat at the kitchen table moping.

“How ‘bout some breakfast, Rick-E?” Spoon asked.

I just shrugged him off.

One thing that’s more uniform in fire stations than the uniforms themselves is most guys give each other nicknames. Take JT for instance. His real name was Charles Dailey but when he first started, he listened to old tapes from James Taylor. Hence the nickname JT. Being that my given name is Rick and last name Edison, the nickname Rick-E was born.

Ramsey walked in and his mood mirrored that of mine. “Yo Ramses, what’s up with you?”

He simply shook his head. Spoon turned around and noticed the difference in him too.

“Come on, man, get some grub. It’s the house special,” Spoon added.

“Naw man,” Ramsey said, barely audible.

Now my concern for Ramsey grew because I have never seen him turn down food. I looked at Spoon, who had just scooped some goulash on his plate. He made a motion to sit down at the table but he must have known that Ramsey needed to talk in private because he swiftly made an about face and went into the day room.

I looked out of the window, waiting for him to tell me what was on his mind. After listening to the sounds of the TV from the adjoining room, I decided to open up the lines of communication.

"Hey man, what's going on with you?"

Ramsey looked up from his coffee cup and glanced around the room.

"Man, life is strange. One day I'm doing OK and the next day, *BAM*, my life is turned upside down."

"What happened?" I asked, genuinely concerned.

"I met a girl."

"You met a girl?"

"Yeah, I met a girl." He then showed off his most brilliant smile. I felt relieved that it wasn't something serious, like cancer.

"What's the big deal about meeting a girl? You met hordes of them already, this is Atlanta, remember?"

"Rick, there's something about her. I mean she's not even fine in the gadunka-dunk sense of the word." He waved his hands in an hourglass shape. "But she makes me feel like I used feel when I was a kid, getting ready for bed on Christmas Eve. You know, that butterfly feeling you got in the pit of your stomach."

"Shit, man, I hadn't had those feelings since the first few months with Shana." I thought about our beginning. My stomach felt giddy when I went to Shana's apartment for dinner. She couldn't cook worth a damn, but just knowing her college roommate was gone, I suffered through the meal, anticipating dessert.

"Then you know what I'm talking about."

I nodded.

He smiled reflectively, "I went to the Big and Tall store in Lenox Mall minding my own business. Tamara was the clerk that helped me. When I tried on a shirt, she straightened up the collar, looked me in the eye and said ever so sweetly, 'You look nice."

"All these professional, well-paid ladies in Atlanta, and you fall for a minimum-wage clerk?"

With the swiftness of a Komodo dragon, Ramsey reached over the table and grabbed my uniform T-shirt. "You always have to put labels on something, you punk ass bitch." He released his grip and kicked the chair.

I felt bad saying that and could have used the kicking instead of the chair. "I'm sorry, man, it's just that when Shana–"

"Don't give me that Shana dying bullshit," he interrupted. "You think you can hide behind that tragedy for the rest of your life. Hell, you were born with a silver spoon up your black ass."

"I'm sorry." I lowered my head and cradled it in my palms. Lately it has been bought to my attention what an absolute asshole I was. No wonder Shana divorced me. I lived two different lives, one at home and another life when I was away from home.

"Sorry. Who am I to judge?"

"You're a friend. I deserved it." I lifted my head and looked at him. "Tell me more about Tamara."

He thought about it for a brief moment and just like that, the bad air between us cleared up. He smiled and began telling me about his new girl. "Like I said, she's not boom-bostic fine, but she is Jackee Harry voluptuous. And sweet as mamma's peach cobbler." He clasped his hands together and sat in deep thought.

"Did you take her out –"

Then it came. The station alarm squealed through the walls of the station, interrupting our conversation. We sprung into action, putting on our bunker gear and headed out. Ramsey drove the truck because JT had a scheduled day off.

Sirens blaring, the engine raced through Atlanta, fighting the horrendous morning rush hour traffic. We took Moreland to North Avenue and through Little Five Points neighborhood.

It was a crossroad of Moreland, Euclid and McLendon Avenues, which in the late twenties flourished as a neighborhood with three movie theaters, several restaurants and shopping for the nearby residents. Little Five Points was to Atlanta then what Buckhead is to the city now. As we approached the Briarcliff Summit, an assisted living high-rise that housed the elderly, I saw black plumes of smoke billowing out of the windows. The building stood on the corner of Ponce and Highland with fifteen stories of elderly. I saw some residents shuffling across the street with walkers, wheelchairs and canes. I shook my head in disgust at the thought of the Federal Government sleeping at night knowing that they confined the elderly to such a potential firetrap. At the sight of more units pulling up and other rigs already there, I knew this was quickly becoming a three-alarm fire.

Patrol cops had cordoned off traffic at the intersection, bringing everything to a dead halt. Ramsey maneuvered the rig closer to the building so the rest of us could jump out and prep it. Cap headed toward the makeshift command post at the Majestic Plaza, across the street. The Majestic Plaza was so old you could still smell the smoke from the likes of Sherman's troops when they burned down Atlanta in 1864. I immediately assumed my duties, connecting the hose from the rig to the hydrant and then feeding the line into the burning building. The hose pumped one hundred gallons of water per minute and got heavy fast. The force of a loose hose at full water pressure could easily decapitate someone. So, skills were involved on my part. Fire fighters from the entire local had arrived, trying to contain the fire, but my gut feeling told me that this baby had to go out on its own.

I looked around and saw elderly men and women walking around in a daze. Over the two-way radio, I heard Cap instruct Ramsey and Spoon to go in and check for survivors. Smelly, the backup nozzle man, helped me anchor the heavy hose. We maneuvered ourselves at the west side of the building. It was almost July in Atlanta and the scorching heat from the sun, coupled with the rising temperature of the burning building, made the flame-resistant bunker gear feel like it was melting against my flesh.

Suddenly, I heard windows shatter as the pressure from the flames forced through the path of least resistance. Then I heard crackling from my radio.

"All units, half-mask on."

I couldn't make out the voice but I was pretty sure it was Cap from the command post. I saw more fire fighters move in the building as people screamed and paranoia set in. I felt helpless holding up the heavy line, but it was my duty and I could not let Smelly take the load by himself.

A scrawny older lady wearing a cotton snap-on duster came up to me. I yelled at her through my mask to get back.

"Sir, I haven't seen Mr. Janson come out," she pleaded in a wispy voice.

Smelly turned and saw her.

"Ma'am, other fire fighters are in there helping the survivors."

"No, you have to help. He's hard of hearing and he's in a wheelchair. I can't help but think that he never heard the alarm."

I had to make a decision. I looked at Smelly and he nodded his head and hoisted the heavy hose over his shoulder to take up the slack when I let go.

I bent down to face the lady. "What apartment is he in?"

"He's on four. Apartment 412."

I grabbed the axe from the rig and jogged toward the building. The closer I got, the hotter it felt. When I reached the main entrance, I heard loud crackling sounds and looked up and saw flames spewing from some of the upper-floor windows. I made it to the main entrance and when I entered the building, I was barely able to see the stairwell sign in the activity room next to the lobby. I opened the heavy oak door and in a matter of seconds I couldn't see anything. Smoke filled the stairwell and there was a tremendous amount of noise adding to my confusion. I jetted up the stairs, counting the flights as I went up. The higher I went, the less I saw.

"Anybody hurt," I yelled out as I made my ascent. I was trained to call out no matter the situation. When I reached the fourth-floor landing, I took off my glove and checked the heat level of the doorknob. Warm but not hot.

When I was positive that there wasn't a backdraft on the other side of the door, I opened it. A thick coat of smoke covered the floor. I turned my helmet light on, though it improved nothing, but I kept it on in hopes that maybe somebody else would see it and call for help.

I started on one side of the floor, feeling my way to the door openings. I counted ten paces between doors. Every ten paces, I strained to see the number on the unit through the thick white smoke. The numbers were raised and I was thankful because I had to feel for apartment 412 due to zero visibility. I found it and again tested for heat on the knob. No monster backdraft behind it, so I turned the knob, only to discover that the door was locked. Running on sheer adrenaline, I swung my axe. After several connections near the knob, I forced my way in the small one-room apartment. A frail man sat in a wheelchair gazing out the window at the fire trucks and commotion. Something told me this man thought the commotion was coming from across the street. I tapped him on the shoulder. When he saw me in the half-mask along with my gear, he took one more look out the window, turned back to me in confusion.

"Come on, let's get you out of here."

I scooped him up and was astonished at his weight. Mr. Janson couldn't have weighed more than ninety pounds. I carried him out the same way I came in, counting paces as I ran. My chest was beginning to tighten as I felt the warm air build up in my lungs. Even though I had on a half mask that filtered the harmful carbon monoxide gases, I still felt the effects in my lungs. But I had to keep going. This was what it was all about, helping others. The only thing that mattered in my life at this moment was returning this feeble man to safety.

I was thankful that I had counted the paces between doors because it helped me navigate to the stairwell. The tightness in my chest kept building. I counted paces, knowing that fresh air was several flights down.

Mr. Janson held on without any particular concern. I heard him cough, so I removed my mask and placed it around his face. I was running on borrowed time.

I made it down two flights of stairs when I heard a loud crash. In the dark, smoke-filled stairwell, I felt a new kind of primal fear, a fear that instinctively I knew would be my last one. Maybe it was true what they say, a coward dies many times but a hero only dies once. I started saying the Lord's Prayer, stumbling on most of the verses.

When I had one flight to go I started coughing hysterically. My stride slowed to a snail's pace and for a moment during that last lag of stairs, I wanted to lie down and sleep. I just wanted to rest and forget all the hurt in my life, all the unjustness in the world and all that I had done to hurt the ones I loved. Suddenly, I heard Dana's voice calling me and I turned around, looking up the stairwell for her. I shook it off and recovered enough energy to get to the lobby. Suddenly I heard another crashing noise, this time louder, and out of the corner of my eye, saw Ramsey carrying two old ladies. We headed out of the building together.

I can't recall the next order of events, but when we made it to the sunlight, I saw several flashes. An instant later, a massive explosion ripped through the tower. The force of the blast propelled Mr. Janson and me through the air at speeds unnatural for the human body. I was flying through the air in slow motion with a hang time of football on return punt. But something wasn't right. I had to protect Mr. Janson. Before my body made impact with the ground, I did a twist in midair so that he would land on me, and not the other way around. The last thing I remembered was the crunching sound in my shoulders as I hit the ground.

I was awakened by the crackling sound of my two-way radio. "I'm trapped in rubble in the stairwell on twelve. Somebody please help." It was Spoon's voice.

When a fellow fire fighter goes down, it feels like alligator jaws clutching down my chest. I tried to get up to run in the building, but the pain in my shoulder sent me back on the pavement. I tried to blink away the pain, but at that moment I couldn't even do that.

I moved my eyes and saw Mr. Janson looking around wildly. One of the elderly ladies Ramsey carried out lay on her side in a fetal position. Ramsey checked her pulse.

"I need a paramedic over here, now!" He raced over to the other lady and helped her up.

Then I heard Spoon again, this time his voice was whisper thin.

"Please, somebody help."

"Hang on, buddy, we're on our way." It was Cap. "Tell me about your contracting business, man. What are you working on tomorrow?"

"Jones Doc um – working at doctor's office on Snapfinger Road and...." Spoon's voice faded out.

Just then Mr. Janson lifted up and ever so lightly tapped me on the shoulder. I simply nodded my head that I was all right. I looked down and saw that my own hands were bloody red from the shrapnel that pierced through the gloves. Funny how I couldn't feel the pain. My pulse raced as I tried to move. I couldn't move any part of my body. I was paralyzed and wished I perished in the explosion instead of facing life in a wheelchair. Ramsey came over and scooped me up.

"How you holding up, buddy?"

"No pain. I'm paralyzed!"

"I'm not a medical expert, but I'd have it's just a broken shoulder blade."

As he carried me to the ambulance, I saw broken glass and metal strewn across the four-lane street. Bloodied survivors and onlookers gazed around, some in a shock-induced trance. Car windows were shattered and some of the windows from nearby buildings were smashed from explosion. The Metro Arson Task Force later reported that their arson dogs sniffed out fire accelerants and ruled the fire as intentional.

Paramedics rushed frantically trying to save lives of fire fighters and the withstanding. I heard more sirens approaching and saw still more plumes of smoke coming from the building. There must have been twenty or so ambulances at the scene. Most were parked in a makeshift hospital zone across the street at the Majestic Plaza. Ramsey dropped me at one where a male paramedic tended to the small cuts from an elderly man.

"I think his shoulder blade is broken," Ramsey said.

"OK, we'll take it from here."

Ramsey took off like a panther on the prowl. Despite my paralysis, I had to smile at Willie Ramsey, he was a trooper. Then I laughed and it turned into a painful, shoulder humping laugh when I remembered one of the guys at the 23rd refer to him as Willie B, the famous Silverback gorilla at the Atlanta Zoo. I felt pain again. The medic noticed me laughing to myself.

"Going into hysteria, uh?" he said, only half joking. He applied pressure to my shoulder blade. "Does this hurt?"

I flinched and have never been so happy to be in pain. I remembered the famous Marine retort, "That hurts very much, thank you, may I have another?"

The medic, a young black man with acne scars, opened up a new plastic syringe. "Are you allergic to anything, penicillin or any type of painkillers?"

"No, just explosions and flying shrapnel."

"I like your attitude. Why don't I give you something for the pain, and then we'll take you to Grady."

"Grady?" I asked, wondering why they would send me there. After he stuck me with the needle, Grady didn't seem all that bad.

11

Grady Memorial Hospital, located in the heart of downtown Atlanta, consisted of a one-thousand-bed facility that was a city in itself. Grady served as the primary hospital for inner-city and medically indigent people in the two largest counties of the Atlanta. It housed the world-renowned Trauma Center, which was vital in the care of patients from the Olympic Park bombing, the Buckhead day trader shootings and the Atlanta Southeast Airway plane crash. No other facility in Atlanta was as capable of handling the volume and acuity of trauma patients as Grady.

I woke up in the hospital's Red Zone, a bay designed for major trauma treatment.

It was full of victims of the Briarcliff Summit fire, and the commotion was at an all-time high. My shoulder was wrapped in a cast and suspended in air by some kind of immobilization device. The wave of pain that encroached my shoulder when I tried to lift was small compared to the alternative. I was alive with feeling, even though it was pain. I looked out the window and thought of Dana's sweet voice at a time I was willing to give up. Then Ramsey carrying me to the ambulance. I had so much to be thankful for. An attending nurse made her way to my bedside.

"Experiencing any pain?" asked the humorless nurse, drawing back the curtain next to my bed.

"Very much."

"We can take care if that." She began the syringe ritual.

"How long have I been out?"

"You broke your collarbone and the doctors sedated you yesterday to keep you immobile."

"I went to surgery?" I asked.

"No, with a collarbone fracture, a brace was used to pull the shoulders back and hold the ends of the bone in line."

"How long will I be out of work?"

"That's up to your doctor, but what I can tell you is that you may or may not have full use of your hand and arms once the pain subsides."

"Umm." Not sure that told me a lot.

She gave me the shot and left me alone. As soon as the medication made its way into my bloodstream and I felt the warmth of the drug take effect, Aisha and Dana walked in.

"Daddy, you are a hero," Dana said as she ran to me and was about to jump on the bed. I said a silent prayer of thanks as Aisha caught her in mid stride with one arm.

"Sweetie, you father's been hurt and you have to be careful."

She placed her down and my sister gave me a worried smile as she unfolded the Atlanta Journal Constitution. The cover, in a seventy-two-point font read: "Local Heroes Save the Elderly, One Perished."

Above the fold was a large picture of me carrying Mr. Janson and Ramsey carrying the two ladies. The photographer, not knowing that an explosion was imminent, must have snapped the picture a nanosecond after the blast, because in the backdrop the approaching explosion with its mushroom-like qualities was in full view. No doubt the photographer would win the National Geographic equivalent prize for best still shot. However, I had no feelings about being a hero because instinctively I knew Spoon had perished.

I lay there, going in and out of consciousness while Dana talked to me. She informed me that Julius was still teasing her and pulling her hair. But when she said she spoke to her mother, I tried to sit up and the pain knocked me back down. I turned to her, giving my undivided attention. "What did you talk about?" I asked, trying to sound nonchalant.

Dana stood on the side of the bed, twisting the hospital sheet. "She looked so pretty and told me that everything is going to be all right."

"What else did she tell you?"

"She told me she loved me and you too."

I lifted my head slightly. "She told you that *I* love you? Don't you know that I do love you?"

Dana stood on her heals and looked down at her feet.

"Dana?"

"When Mommie told me you loved me, I called out for you and you didn't come."

"She was having a bad dream and woke up crying for you," Aisha offered.

"When was this?"

"Yesterday morning, why?"

I turned away so they couldn't see the tears welling up. When I turned back to Dana, I grabbed her little hand with my good hand. "Baby, I want you to remember that I will always love you, no matter what." I gently bought her hand to my lips and kissed it. "Would you remember that for Daddy?"

"OK. When you get out of he hospital, can you take us to Six Flags?"

"That's a date." Kids have the resiliency of a rubber band, bouncing back quickly.

After Dana and Aisha left, they moved me from the trauma ward to my private room, where a parade of well-wishers visited me. Even Mayor Shirley Franklin marched in with a camera crew on her heels. Outside my door, she gave a scripted speech about the fire department's courage.

I was amazed when I saw Ramsey. Not only was he up and walking, but also did he not have a visible scar on his body.

"I guess a brother has to break a collarbone before the Mayor visits."

"Don't hate the player, hate the game."

Ramsey let out one of his shrieking laughs and I felt more at ease when I heard it. "How are you feeling?"

"I can't really tell. These narcotics are great."

"Did you see the newspaper?"

"Yeah, Aisha bought in a copy." I turned and looked out the window and thought about Mathew Witherspoon. "I don't feel like much of a hero."

"Yeah, I know what you mean."

"Where did they find him?"

"Why don't you worry about recovering instead?"

"It should've been me in there and not him. I mean, he was getting his life on track, sober and all." I paused, fighting back the tears. Too many people around me were dying and I was not able to do a damn thing about it. "I just don't understand why God chose him instead of an asshole like me."

"Man, don't beat up on yourself. You risked your life to save that old man." He paused for effect. "That's why God put you here."

"Willie Ramsey, what's with the newfound spirituality?"

"After seeing all those frail old people, I question my own existence. Then Tamara explained to me how we don't need to understand God's will. She told me that more will be revealed."

"Umm. Dana told me she talked to Shana and she said that everything will be all right."

"I don't doubt it. They say the very young and very old can see spirits."

"I am a believer."

Ramsey took a seat in the recliner next to the bed. "What's going on with the picture of the guy from Emory? I meant to ask yesterday before the fire."

"That's right, I haven't given you the latest." I looked up at the ceiling, trying to recall where I left off with Ramsey. When I collected my thoughts, I told him about the meeting with Durden McDeevil and the subsequent photo. I told him how I went to Dr. Van Hart and asked her for a craniofacial identification.

"Craniofacial identification?"

"Man, technology is incredible. Aisha told me about this Discovery Channel special on the replication of human-like face from a skull."

"But you don't have a skull."

"That's why I went to talk to Van Hart. Durden said that it's possible to get a three-dimensional model from a still."

"What are you going to do if you get a face?"

"That, I don't know. Maybe I'll hang out at Five Points MARTA station until I see him."

"Or maybe not."

"I took your advice and gave Lisa a visit at the CDC."

"What she say? She gonna help?"

"She said I was an asshole."

"She could've told you something you didn't already know." He swung at my shoulder blade and I winced right before he pulled back.

On the day of my release from the hospital, Fire Chief Breman, a short, dumpy man with flawless white skin, shocked me by visiting my room. The captain and lieutenant of the 23rd joined him. Since there were no cameras around, as had been the case with Mayor Franklin, the visit was a compliment.

"Son, I understand you have an attendance problem," Breman said. His voice was twice his size, and I wondered how he passed the physical training test that was mandatory for all fire fighters.

I looked wildly at Cap, not sure I understood his definition of 'attendance problem.' "Sir I haven't called in sick once during my career. Not even when my wife died did I take the entire leave."

"That's what I'm talking about." He roared with laughter that was so contagious that we all joined in. "Son, you did a fine job of rescue at Briarcliff Summit and I'm telling you – no, demanding you – to take the required six weeks off."

I turned to Cap for help. I couldn't stay home for six weeks for a broken collarbone. I was going bat shit crazy with the investigation while working. "Chief, I – um don't think I need all that time. It's just a broken collarbone. The doctor said I could still use my hand."

Breman looked at Cap. "You warned me about him." Then he turned to me. "Listen, son, I need you to recuperate for me. You are a hot item with the press and I don't need you to as much as get a paper cut while on my watch. So take some vacation. That's an order."

"But that leaves two openings with me and Spoon." As soon as I said it,

I felt the atmosphere in the room tense.

"Let us handle the headcount," Lt. Anderson said. "I'll take your tour until you come back and Human Resources will secure us another body."

Depending on the county, each station had a captain on every shift and one lieutenant who mans the business side of the house. In most cases, the lieutenant took responsibility for more than one station, and in Anderson's case, he had three. He usually worked seven in the morning to four in the afternoon, Monday through Friday.

"Besides, you'll be in that sling for a while," Cap said.

I looked down at my right arm in the simple triangular sling and had to agree.

"We want you back at one hundred percent." The chief saluted me and they filed out of the small room. I paced the floor, waiting for the nurse to come with the release papers and caddy. No matter what the injury, hospitals did not let patients walk out on their own.

Ramsey met me outside and drove me home. Despite the fact that I had slept more in the last two days than I had in a long while, I felt dizzy and slightly nauseated. When he turned a sharp right, my first instinct told me to grab the handle, but my right hand was literally tied up.

"What are you gonna do with yourself, boy?" Ramsey asked as he headed down Butler Street.

"Boy? You better feel again," I chided him. "I have no clue what I am going to do for six weeks." This felt like a lie in light of the investigation, but I felt too weak to get into it right now. "Man, tell me something. How in the hell did you escape any injury after the explosion?"

"Only God knows."

"When is Spoon's funeral?"

"Saturday."

"Saturday? That's almost a week from now."

"Yeah, you know how us black folks are. We'll ice the body down until Ree Ree and 'nem can make it."

We shared a hearty laugh, and I felt tendrils of pain race up and down my shoulder.

"I know that's right."

When he dropped me off in front of my unit, I hesitated before opening the door. "Life is just too short. You never know when your number is coming up."

"You got that right. That's why I'm going to ask Tamara to marry me."

"What! Are you serious?"

"Yes indeed, and I want you to meet her."
"Anytime and anyplace."

Mathew Witherspoon's closed casket graveside service was a heartfelt one held at Wake Forest Memorial Gardens in Southwest Atlanta. Mayor Shirley Franklin gave the eulogy as the most of the county's several hundred fire fighters listened in mourning. I saw several women fire fighters and had neither ill will nor accolades for them. They were just fire fighters. There was an emotionally felt seven-gun salute. I took it all in and felt eerie to be at a funeral so close to Shana's, especially since his death was ruled a homicide.

I learned that Spoon's body had been pulled from the rubble of one of the higher floors. With other floors toppling over him, his body was so unrecognizable the medical examiner was astounded that he was able to call for help moments before his death. Miraculously, none of the Briarcliff Summit residents lost their lives. There were about twelve fire fighters, EMS workers and police officers and two civilians treated for minor injuries, ranging from smoke inhalation to cuts and bruises.

The repast was held at the World Changers Church in College Park. World Changers was a non-denominational church sitting on a sprawling ninety-two-acre campus with five thousand members. The reverend informed us that repast was another name for fried chicken after a funeral. Rumor has it that he offered to take care of the repast in order to recruit more souls.

I had an opportunity to meet Tamara there. She wasn't anything like I imagined. The gold-clad hoochie-mama with long curvy nails and a wrapped ponytail that I had imagined turned out to be a woman who carried herself with the class and dignity not found in retail professionals in Atlanta. She was heavyset, but it fit her. She wore light bouts of makeup to be appropriate and styled her hair in an a-line bob. I liked her and wanted to be in her company. Good for Ramsey, I thought, and gave him a wink.

The days afterwards were filled with game shows in the morning, trash in the afternoon and mind-numbing sitcoms in the evening. I found myself taking the pain medication, Percocet, even when the pain had dulled. It was a way to escape the monotony of the day. I was so bored that I finally snapped out of it and decided to head downtown.

I made it there in twenty minutes, driving with my good arm, and found a parking spot near the Grady statue on Marietta. I looked forward to talking with Doc and didn't really know why. When I entered the shoe bar, I took a seat at one of the barstools. Doc was hard at work hammering a new three-inch heel on a J. Renee shoe.

"How ya' doing, Doc?"

"If I was doing any better, I'd be in heaven." He turned at looked at me. "Say, what happened to your arm, son?"

I felt a warm calm when he called me son. My father died of sickle cell anemia when I was very young and I never got a chance to get to know him. My rearing was shared between my mother, who worked two jobs, and my grandmother, who stayed at home and instilled fear in our hearts. Big Mama, as Aisha and I called her, stood stern on her beliefs that children should obey their elders. When I accidentally called her neighbor Marvin instead of Mr. Fields, she popped me on the head with a hairbrush and said, "Boy don't call adults by their first name, you'd better put a handle on it." I looked at Doc with a closed-lipped smile.

"I guess you heard about the fire on the news."

"Don't watch the news. Too much negative sensationalism, all of it."

"Did you read the newspaper about the fire at Briarcliff Summit?"

"Don't read the papers, either."

"How do you stay abreast of current events?"

"People like you tell me." He finished with the J. Renee heel and walked to the same side of the counter that I sat on. "What happened?"

"Mathew Witherspoon was killed in the explosion and I got this souvenir." I held out my sling.

Doc gazed down and clenched his fist. "Damn, damn, damn!"

I turned to look out the window at the cars and pedestrians passing and couldn't help but to think of Florida Evans on *Good Times* when she got the telegram that James was dead. I remained silent and it was Doc who spoke first.

"When I first met him the day he painted your office, I got a whiff of alcohol on his breath. When I told him that I was a member of AA for nearly twenty years, he asked me how I did it." Doc now gazed out of the window, his eyes glassy. "I simply told him that I did it one day at a time."

"So it was you?"

I sat and talked with Doc for twenty minutes or so. He ranted on about AA and I listened. I went upstairs to look at the tapes one last time. Maybe I would catch something that I missed, but when I arrived at the office, I saw just four more walls staring at me and sighed at my boredom. What do the unemployed do day after day?

I sat down at the desk, careful not to hit my arm on the corner, and went to put a tape in. It didn't matter which one I grabbed, so I picked up the first one I touched. When I went to insert the tape in the AMC, I saw the phone and remembered that I needed to check the voicemail at the apartment. When I dialed the mailbox number and entered the password, the mechanical lady told me I had seven new messages. Two were from Dana while I was in the hospital. The third message worried me.

It was Lisa Merriwether. "I saw your picture in the paper and – well, give me a call when you get this."

I hung up the phone without checking the other messages. What did she want? I was reluctant to call because I didn't want any bad news. I yanked the phone from its cradle and dialed the number she left. I thought she'd given me her number at the CDC but it must have been her cell phone, because when she answered it, she said hello.

"Hey, this is Rick."

"Bring me the toxicology report and I'll look it over."

I held the phone out and looked at it. "What's with the change of heart?"

"Let's just say I know the granddaughter of Mr. Janson, Mr. Hero," she said and let out a chuckle.

"Thanks, Lisa."

"Oh, you're gonna thank me all right. Meet me at the Louis Vuitton shop in Lenox at five thirty."

After pacing the office waiting on five thirty to get here, going from looking out of the window to looking at the visitors and employees on the surveillance tapes, I left the office on my way to Lenox Mall. I walked to the car and the humidity along with the painkillers wore me out.

When I turned the corner onto Peachtree, my cell phone rang. This put me in a precarious situation, as I my arm was still in a sling and I couldn't hold the steering wheel with one hand and grab the phone with the other, I had to pull over in the Army surplus store parking lot in order to answer it.

"Hello."

"Rick, this is Dr. Van Hart. I have something for you."

When it rained it poured. One moment I was watching *Jerry Springer* and *Texas Justice*, and the next moment I had to be in two places at one time.

"Can I come by in a couple of hours?"

"I'd rather not meet here. Where are you? I can come there, because this is pretty interesting."

I thought quickly. "How about I treat you to a nice steak dinner for your time? My way of saying thanks."

"That sounds like something I can sink my teeth into."

I caught the pun. "We're in a good mood."

"I'd have to say so. The replica is so lifelike. I tell you what, why don't I take some color photos and bring them with me?"

"How about meeting me at Morton's Steak House in Buckhead at seven thirty?"

"I'll be there. And Rick, don't forget your promise."

I glanced at my watch and noticed it was approaching five thirty. I had to make it to Lenox, then get home to shower and change for the dinner meeting with Dr. Van Hart. Out of curiosity, I called the restaurant and asked if they required reservations.

As it turned out, reservations were not only suggested, but also they were required. While I had the maître-d' on the phone, I asked him to chill their best bottle of Merlot.

He hesitated. "Sir, may I suggest the Merlot be served at room temperature, as its natural flavor is best revealed?" he offered in a haughty tone.

I am not sure how anyone can drink warm red wine, but where I come from, we chill ours and sometimes put it over ice. "If it's all right with you, I'd like to have it chilled."

"Very well, sir."

I met Lisa at the Louis Vuitton boutique and was coaxed into buying her a three-hundred-dollar purse for her efforts. Women paid too much money for purses. We exchanged goods and left. I made it home in time to take a decent shower and change into my tan linen dinner jacket with my cream-colored summer wool pants. I felt a rush of excitement as I changed in the neatly laundered clothes and had someplace nice to go. I just wish I had enough time to get the Expedition detailed, but that had to wait because I was pressed for time.

12

Morton's Steakhouse had more cuts of beef than the law allowed. I rushed in and took a seat at the huge mahogany bar that sat in the center of the refined restaurant. The elegant décor offered a country-club atmosphere, both classic with the white linen tablecloths, and romantic with the soft candlelit tables.

Dr. Van Hart met me at the bar and we were promptly seated at a high-back corner booth. She wore an elegant, after-six Vera Wang knock-off with high-heeled patent leather sandals. She also wore a tasteful layer of makeup, and seeing her with it on for the first time, I thought she looked like Stephanie Mills.

While we looked over the menu, the tuxedo-clad waiter came over with the Merlot and removed the cork from the bottle and handed it to me. I sniffed it and nodded my head. He then poured a small amount in my wineglass, at which point I picked it up, swirled it around and took a sip, as I had seen in the movies. After I nodded again, he filled both glasses to three-quarters.

We especially enjoyed Morton's tableside menu presentation, when the waiter rolled a cart of steaks, lobsters and other main selections, along with fresh vegetables and described each item in an appetizing and entertaining detail. I ordered the fourteen-ounce, double-cut filet, and she chose the Chicken Christopher in garlic beurre blanc sauce.

"I take it you've been here before?" she asked over a sip of wine.

"I've always wanted to come here, but thought it was too expensive."

"You didn't have to bring me here. I'll help pay."

"Dr. Van Hart, you took your personal time to help me with the photo and I wanted to do something nice for you."

She smiled, "Call me Teri."

I felt uneasy all of a sudden, and I thought I needed to give an explanation. "The guys took up a collection for me after my wife was um – well, you know. And I haven't had time to spend it yet."

Van Hart nodded. The atmosphere had not changed her entirely. When she spoke again, she was back to business. "Speaking of which, have the police found any new leads in your wife's murder investigation?"

I paused, thinking over what she just said. "Actually, she was my ex-wife. The divorce was final two days before she was murdered."

"Oh, I see."

The waiter interrupted us as he bought our dinner. While we ate, Van Hart explained how she had mapped the algorithms to come up with a 3-D dataset. She then went on to explain the tediousness of the facial approximation from the skull, measurements of distances, angles and areas and how she used the conventional multivariate technique. As she talked, I bit into my double-cut filet and couldn't believe the taste. It was a cut of pure heaven.

Overall, she was satisfied with the end product, and I wanted to see it, but she kept eating. As soon as we finished our entrees, the waiter came over and removed our plates. Out of the corner of my eye, I saw him talk with the maître-d' and nod his head in our direction. For a brief moment, I felt out of place.

I played with the linen napkin. "Have you ever seen such a brutal murder in your career?"

"Rick, people can be very cruel and inherently evil." She raised her glass of Merlot and took a long swallow. "Five or so years back, I autopsied a case where a nine-year-old girl fatally stabbed her abusive father."

"That doesn't seem so brutal."

"Until you count one hundred and thirty-eight stab wounds. With an insulin syringe."

I shook my head in disgust. "How can a child become so embodied with evil?"

"The little girl had been repeatedly raped so much by him that her vagina was stretched to the size of a woman who had given birth."

I swallowed hard. "If anyone did that to my daughter, I'd be more than willing to serve jail time for his murder."

She reached underneath the table and removed a manila envelope from her purse. Hesitantly, she slid it across the table. I felt it in my hands, envisioning him in the death chamber as the men pulled the switch, savoring thoughts of justice that would soon come. Was I prepared to see the monster who killed my wife? My curiosity got the better of me, and I slowly removed one of the pictures from the envelope, staring at it in disbelief. In my naïveté, I was expecting a real-life photo of a man with real skin and real eyes. Instead, I saw a partial view of a bust-like mold of a man's head. The Neanderthal-looking creature stared out with a one-dimensional gaze. I brought the picture closer and noticed that his skin was plastered with some kind of clay-like substance that made his complexion look waxy and hardened. It looked so otherworldly that I had to bat my eyelids to keep my sensory functions focused. I pulled out the next photo and saw a full frontal shot. I noticed that the bridge of his nose bulged out and threatened to overwhelm the rest of his features. But the eyes – I was drawn to their expressionless disposition. Dolls had more life in their eyes than he did.

I looked up at Van Hart, speechless.

"Remember, facial reconstruction is not a means of positive identification, just a way of creating a likeness to confirm an identity."

"But I thought–"

"You thought it was going to be an bona-fide individual. You have to take in account this is my first time."

"I'm sorry – I didn't mean to imply that what you did was bad." I scratched my head. "I just thought I'd have something more concrete to take to the police." I looked at the photo again. "By the way, how did you come up with the eye and hair color?"

"Since I didn't have any DNA samples, I had to use what we in the medical field call an educated guess. By the fact that he took an effort to hide his natural hair color with a black wig, I surmised that he wasn't a brunette."

"That listens. But why not a redhead?"

"Since most men don't purposely dye their hair red and his features don't signify the contours of a natural redhead, I guessed him to be light to medium blond."

"What do you mean?"

She got more animated with that question. "Studies from several medical journals reveal that natural redheads have flat nose bridges and smaller lower jaws. Plus, most redheads have fair skin and the original photo you gave me from the video surveillance had a medium skin tone."

The waiter came around and presented the dessert cart in the same fashion as the main menu selections. After we both declined, he left a thin American Express tray with the bill on it.

"A lot of work went into this," I said, looking at the bastard who sodomized and killed her. But why did he pick Shana? I had to find the connection.

"I treated the project like a map and distinguished features by numerology."

"Oh, that's all," I said, trying to relieve the stress that had consumed me. As soon as I took the last sip from my wine, I noticed a snooty lady at the next table looking over at me. "What the hell are you looking at," I yelled in her direction.

"Rick, what are you doing?" Van Hart snapped.

I bowed my head, not knowing what came over me. "I'm so frustrated I don't know what I'm doing anymore." The lady at table turned away from our table. I felt like shit.

"You need to control yourself. You cannot go through life like you're the only one here." She cut her eyes away from me and reached for her purse.

"Please don't go." I was at a loss.

She let go of her purse and thought out her next words. "You ruined my viewing glass at the morgue, you got yourself arrested–"

"That wasn't my fault."

"Oh, it wasn't. Didn't you tell me they had a tape of you threatening your wife?"

"Yes."

"Well, there you go," she said, waving me off. "Get control of your temper and take it easy. Why do you have to find the killer tonight?"

"Because he's walking the streets a free man."

She grabbed my hand, commanding my full attention. "Rick, you're on the right track. You have more than the police and you might be closer than you think. Just take your time, OK?" She released my hand and gave me a smile.

"You think I'll find him?"

"With your tenacity, I think you can find Bin Laden, if given a chance."

I smiled at her and felt better about the investigation. I just had to take my time. "Thanks, Doctor."

"What are you going to do with the pictures?"

"I'm going to go over all the evidence and take my time."

When I removed the bill, there was a zero balance and a note, 'Compliments of Morton's Steakhouse for your bravery at Briarcliff Summit.' I felt undeserving of a complimentary meal, especially after bawling out the lady at the next table. So when Van Hart and I passed the maître-d', I slid him two one-hundred-dollar bills, asking him to take care of that table's meal.

On the lonesome drive home, I glanced at the pictures that rested on the passenger seat and wondered how was I going to identify the zombie-like man. Then I thought of Kimi and the AJC's database of known criminals. I pulled over in the parking lot at Zesto's in order to call her. I was getting used to the sling, but some moves required extra effort. When I reached for my phone, it rang. I wondered who was calling me.

"Hello."

"This is Sheila from Emory. I can't talk long, but it was Marlene Kennard." She hung up.

I stared straight ahead, dumfounded. Who the hell was Sheila from Emory? *Sheila from Emory.* I wanted to pound my frustrations out on the steering wheel but I remembered Van Hart's words. I took in a couple of deep breaths and relaxed. Slowly, it came to me. She was the nurse at Emory. Why had she changed her mind, I wondered, and thought of the free meal at Morton's. Maybe Sheila saw the picture in the paper. Perhaps being a hero isn't as bad as I thought it'd be.

Shana was visiting Marlene Kennard the night of the murder. That name sounded familiar, but I couldn't place where I heard it. I called Kimi and told her the good news. She said she'd come by the office in the morning.

Kimi came by the office a little before nine with two cinnamon raisin bagels and two cups of chocolate macadamia nut coffee. I enjoyed her company and as usual, she was dressed immaculate, wearing a navy blue Ralph Lauren crescent jacket with the matching pants. She sat on the couch, eating her breakfast, and I noticed how the sunlight caught the gold hues of her hazel eyes.

As she ate, she looked over the pictures. "This is amazing. Can I include your contact's name in the article?"

"What article?"

"The exclusive story, remember?"

"Now I remember why you are being so nice to me."

"And don't you forget it, either." She took the last bite of her bagel for emphasis. "I'll run this by our database and see what I come up with."

After she left, I couldn't help but chuckle about her. She was the type of woman that could intimidate a man at first sight by her beauty and independence. But the more I got to know her, the more at ease I felt around her.

Just then, I was jolted out of my daydream by a knock at the door. I got up and saw that it was Ramsey.

"What's up?"

"I thought you would be here. I need your help," Ramsey said, letting himself in.

I looked at him, wondering what was wrong. "Just name it and claim it, man."

"I'm proposing to Tamara tonight and I want you to help me."

"How do I go about helping you propose to *your* girlfriend?"

"Well, since you been married before, I was hoping you'd show me how to do it."

"Rams, proposing ain't like French kissing, I can't show you how to do it. Just get down on one knee and ask her to marry you." I went back to my seat at the desk. "Do you have the ring?"

"What ring? I thought I needed that on the wedding day."

"Oh boy." I sighed. "The engagement ring is the most important thing to a woman. It's the one they show off while they make wedding plans."

"Wedding plans?"

"Yes, wedding plans. Things like the location of the ceremony, menu for the reception, guest list and honeymoon details are wedding plans."

"I think I'll wait," he said as if deciding not to order dessert. "What's going on with the mystery man?" And just like that, Ramsey called off the engagement.

I just looked at him. His simplicity boggled my mind. I shook my head and got him up to speed on the latest developments. I told him about the craniofacial identification that Van Hart reconstructed and how Kimi was running it against the newspaper's database of known criminals.

"She was able to do it?" Ramsey asked with a squinted face.

"Yes, and as a matter of fact," I reached over and pulled out one of the pictures of the mystery man, "here he is."

He studied the pictures with astute intent. "So this is the man at the hospital who ducked all the camera angles?"

"That's the one."

"He looks a little like JT's bald-headed ass."

"Oh, and another thing," I said, disregarding his last statement. "I found out who Shana was seeing at the hospital anyway."

"Yeah, who was it?"

"Marlene Ken–" I jumped out of my seat, almost snagging the sling on the desk. "Marlene Kennard, Ramsey. She's one of Shana's patients." I made my way around the desk to go downstairs and get the box with Shana's personal belongings. The phone rang.

"Hello," I almost yelled into the phone.

"Rick, I have bad news for you." It was Kimi.

"More bad news," I said and threw up my hand.

"Yeah, unfortunately, we have no matches to anyone in our database."

"You've got to be kidding me?"

"No. I'm sorry. Look, maybe I can check with Durden to see if he can do the same."

"Never mind, Kimi. I might've found something else. I'll call you later." I clicked the phone off and headed for the door.

"Who was that?"

"That was Kimi. She didn't find anything. Not a damn thing."

I went to my SUV and got the box of personal belongings I collected from Shana's office. I had a hard time trying to close the door with the box in my good hand and my other arm in the sling. Oh what the hell, it had been a while since I felt pain in my shoulder, so I flung off the sling and let my arm drop to its natural position. I made it back upstairs and sat the box on the desk. I had forgotten about the personal belongings and the laptop. It remained in the SUV the entire time and I guessed that the computer's circuitry was blown from the heat. I pulled it out and booted it up.

"What's in the computer?"

"That's what I intend to find out."

I was able to boot it and retrieve her personal folder. I went directly to Marlene's file. I didn't understand hardly any of its contents, especially the diagnosis of major depressive disorder. I saw that Marlene had suffered from acute weight loss, loss of interest in pleasure and abnormal fatigue.

Ramsey glanced at me. "You think she did it?"

"Patients have been known to kill their doctors."

We both remained silent as the sounds of the city echoed in the background.

"Let's go talk to Marlene Kennard," I said as I went through the folder and got the address.

13

To my surprise, Marlene Kennard lived in the Bluff, a rough section of town where the very poor and the very addicted lived. Stories of the area went back to the sixties, when heroin found its way from the Vietnam ghettos to mainstream Atlanta. It's rumored that white people traveled from the suburbs to the slums of the Bluff to score high-potency heroin. Located directly east of downtown, the section of town was landscaped with ransacked bungalow houses and a mesh of low-rent apartments. North Avenue, where Coca-Cola housed their worldwide headquarters, ran directly into English Avenue, the heart of the seedy area, where you can buy any quantity of the brown powder. The Bluff was of a grid of Simpson, Northside, Bankhead and Ashby, the worst streets in Atlanta where inside these invisible walls, was a tress of unspeakable crimes and death due to overdose. On any given Friday or Saturday night, the area came alive with zombie-like fiends in search of the next big hit.

Driving through the neighborhood gave me a grave sense of apprehension as I saw vacant eyes, watching us, casing us. I felt like raw meat on display at a New York butcher shop. I was catapulted in another time and place, not understanding why Marlene, who had a good job with MARTA, would live in hell's jungle.

We found the address from the file and parked in front of the painted clapboard house with a crow's nest attic. The house next door was boarded up and the lot was scattered with years of litter. We were silent on the way to the house and I took the folder in an attempt to look official. I just wanted to question her about that night, maybe she'd lead me in some direction, any direction.

Before I rang the doorbell, Ramsey looked at me pensively and I wondered what that look meant. When I pushed it, I didn't hear anything inside. We waited for what seemed like an hour, and people were watching us. The neighborhood was so ominous that a part of me was relieved that no one was home. Maybe we'd try her at MARTA.

Then a spindly man in his mid-thirties muddled to the door. The first thing I noticed as he kicked the screen door open was his boots. They were the ostrich boots that looked like peanut brittle. The sour stench of his alcohol-laden breath came through the screen door. When I looked up at his face, I gasped so deeply that my jaw dropped. My body stood there motionless as I saw the exact likeness to the craniofacial mold Van Hart had constructed. I turned my eyes towards Ramsey and judging from his expression, he recognized the resemblance. The words I wanted to say to this spineless coward escaped me. I wanted to rip his head off with my bare hands and at the same time I wanted him alive to find out why he killed Shana.

His stony expression went from unyielding to contempt, as we stood there speechless. "The hell do you boys want?"

My mind tore through mixed emotions. I had to think fast. "Sir, have you accepted Jesus Christ as your Lord and personal savior?" I belted out in my best TV evangelist impression, tapping the folder for emphasis.

Marlene Kennard's husband hesitated, looking us over with blazing eyes. "Get the hell off my property, you Jesus freaks." He released the screen door and slammed it shut.

A wave of relief washed over me, as I have never felt so good about getting a door slammed in my face. Ramsey and I lumbered to the 4Runner, and it wasn't until we left the quadrant of the Bluff that either of us spoke.

"I can't believe we found him. I could've shit my pants when I got a good look at his face." Ramsey's big chest heaved up and down from the adrenaline rush.

"I haven't been sure of a lot of things in my life, but I am sure about knowing he killed my wife." I looked out of the window, biting my knuckles.

"What are you going to do now?"

"I'm going to the police, that's what I'm going to do."

"Good idea. How did you come up with the Jesus scam so fast?"

"Rams, that guy scared the living shit out of me. When I saw his face, I knew he had killed before and probably will do it again." I sat silent, thinking about those words. "A man like that definitely doesn't want God in his life."

I have never been afraid of another man. Hell, in my younger days, I sincerely thought I could beat Mike Tyson, but Kennard scared me shitless. "We're going to hand this over to the police and give Kimi the story, then I'm out of it."

"I'm supposed to meet Tamara tonight."

"Oh." I felt deflated. We worked hard to find the killer and now he wanted to spend time with his lady.

Ramsey dropped me off at the office, and I immediately got in my SUV and drove to the East Precinct. I didn't care if the smug desk sergeant made me wait two hours; I was bound and determined to talk to Leicky. True enough, he was behind the counter and when I asked for Leicky, his attitude had changed.

"Let me call them for you." He picked up the rotary phone. "Want some coffee or something?"

I frowned, wondering what kind spirit got hold of him. "Naw, I'll be all right."

I was immediately passed through and walked up to homicide division. Leicky and Biddings were at their desk along with most other detectives, though they didn't gape at me like before.

"Local hero saves the elderly." Biddings stood up and clapped his hands in a slow, obnoxious rhythm.

I wanted to pounce on him like a cat on catnip but instead I gave him a sneer and said, "It wasn't me." It's bad enough when fire fighters get caught on TV and have to endure other fire fighters' jokes, but having the likes of Biddings chastise me about doing my job was why I avoided cameras.

"I read the article," he said back with a you-idiot tone.

"Oh, they taught you to read in special ed?" I replied, and the room erupted in laughter by the other detectives who made no attempts to shroud their disgust for Biddings.

Leicky rubbed his forehead. "So, Mr. Edison, what's on your mind today?"

"I'd like an update on the murder investigation," I said, keeping my hold card until I found out what they knew.

Leicky looked up at the ceiling and sighed. "In an open investigation, we are not required to give out information."

"She was my wife, Leicky. Why can't I know?"

He looked down between his legs and I caught a glimpse of sorrow.

"You closed the investigation, didn't you?"

"No, an investigation is never closed until the perp is found."

"Then what is it?"

He hesitated longer than I wanted him to.

"We don't have the file and until we find time in our sixty-hour workweek to retake statements from the hospital employees and get another crime scene unit out there then, the investigation has been pushed back."

"Pushed back where?" I asked, eyes bulging wildly.

"Inactive status."

"What does that mean, inactive?"

"It means we don't have a damned thing, OK? Is that what you want to hear from us?" Leicky stood up. "We lost the file and fucked up. Now there, I said it."

"We have him." Biddings looked at Leicky for approval.

"Shut the fuck up, Larry," Leicky snarled at him. "You know, if you started pulling your weight around here, instead of being a narrow-minded prick, maybe we wouldn't have lost the damn file."

There was a hush that came over the room, as I noticed that the other detectives' heads were buried in their work. As much as I loathed Biddings, I felt sorry for him. He had taken the burden of responsibility for the stolen file. A part of me wanted to confess but I kept quiet, enjoying Biddings' discomfort. I thought about walking away and checking into hiring a private investigator, but they, too, needed the resources of the police department. I decided to bring out my hold card.

I explained about the mystery man on the surveillance tapes to Leicky, as well as the connection at CNN who transcoded the video format to an image, and the craniofacial identification. I concluded by telling him that Marlene Kennard was the patient Shana visited that night.

Leicky leaned back in his chair and crossed his arms over his chest. "You've probably broken more laws than I care to write up."

I rolled my eyes at him in disgust. Here I was handing him leads and he threatened me. I ignored him for the moment and continued, "I went to see Marlene and her husband answered the door." I sat in silence, proud of my accomplishment.

"And?" Biddings asked sharply.

"And, he's the man at the hospital."

Leicky sat up in his chair. "So what you're telling me is that you discovered a man at the hospital, the same hospital where his wife was a patient?"

"Yes. Don't you see the connection?"

"No, I don't."

I looked over at Biddings and for the life of me I don't know why. Then I gave my best please-understand-what-I-am-trying-to-say look to Leicky. He simply shrugged.

I stood up and paced the walkway between the rows of desks. "One, Shana was murdered at the hospital and this Kennard man knew she would be there." I sat down and grabbed a Post-It note pad from Leicky's desk. "That's opportunity." I wrote that down and stuck it on the edge of his desk. Then I got up again, using my hands for additional emphasis. "Two, Marlene's husband didn't want her seeing a psychologist." I made it back to the Post-It pad. "That's motive!" I jotted that down and placed it next to the first note.

"You knew she was there, too," Biddings said maliciously.

"Look, I'm trying to help find the bastard who murdered my wife. I'm not selling little kids crack, I'm not killing innocent people, and hell, I even pay my taxes. Can I get just a minute of your unbiased cooperation?"

This time Biddings stood up and got in my face. "You want motive? How's this, your wife divorces you and takes your only child? That's motive. And–"

"That's enough, Larry."

"No, Bill, I'm sick of this pompous ass-clown coming in our shop, telling us how to do our jobs. You don't see me at the fire station telling him how to run a hose."

By this time the entire homicide division turned and faced us.

"Let's not forget opportunity. When you called her and threatened her life, she told you she was on her way to the hospital. We have it on tape, remember?" He opened his lap drawer, removed a miniature answering machine tape and waved it like it was a winning lottery ticket. "That's opportunity."

"If I murdered my wife, why would I bust my ass trying to find her killer?"

"That's simple. To throw us off the scent."

"Throw you off what scent? Hell, you all but closed the case. If I killed her, I'd be home free, according to the Atlanta Police Department."

Leicky rubbed his head and looked at both of us. He looked disgusted, not only with Biddings, but also with me. "Both of you listen to me. First, I'll give your findings to the lieutenant and see if we can get some help with the file. And second, I want you to stay out of the way." He gave me a stern look.

"I'll be glad to stay out of the way, once you get in the way." I stood to leave. Leicky followed me and remained silent until we reached the elevator bank. I pressed the down button and waited, feeling awkward.

"You did a good job, thanks." He looked away from me. I raised my eyebrow, not sure how I felt about that comment.

"I just hope you can use it."

I sat around the apartment the next day, waiting for Leicky to call me with news of the arrest. I tried to watch television, but that didn't lower my anticipation. I thought about going to a bar but I remembered the police escort from my last drunken outing. I tried to call Ramsey, but he switched his cell phone off when he was with Tamara. I called Dana, but it seemed her social calendar had no place for me either. I felt lonely and sorry for myself. The only thing I had to look forward to was my follow-up doctor's visit. I had to find a way to get an early release to go back to work.

14

After begging my doctor for an early release, I returned to work three weeks earlier. I was met with an onslaught of good cheer and adulation, even JT seemed happy about my return. One of the guys even had framed a copy of the newspaper picture and hung it up in the day room. I left the guys watching *Good Day Atlanta* and headed to the bunkroom to drop my duffel bag. When I crossed the threshold, what I saw sent me careening back to the day room.

Cap, JT and Ramsey were still sitting there watching television.

"What's up with the new construction in the bunkroom?" I asked referring to a remolded section that was once an open room with eight twin-sized beds.

"Oh, that's right, you haven't heard," Cap spoke up." We have a new fire fighter on B shift."

I looked at Ramsey then back at Cap. "I don't get it."

"Oh, you will, my friend, you will," Cap smiled.

There was undercurrent of snickers. I looked at Ramsey, upset that he didn't tell me and turned his head to hide from my questioning look. "Would somebody please tell me what's going–"

I noticed that Cap was looking over my shoulder. When I turned to see what he was staring at, I felt my face get hot. Standing in the entryway to the day room was a mother-of-all, gorgeous woman, lips full as Gladys Knight and creamy smooth skin. She had hips like an onion, made a man want to cry. She was absolutely fine. And to top it off, she wore a fire fighter's uniform. I was speechless.

"Naia Jordan, I want you to meet Rick. Rick Edison, the 23rd's newest hero."

"Cap, come on." I looked at him and grimaced while blushing inside. I extended my hand to Naia.

"Nice to meet you," she said softly as she extended her hand. "I wish it wasn't under these circumstances."

I don't know if it was my imagination but she held on to my hand a second longer than the norm, and I could have sworn I saw that familiar look of seduction.

"So – um how long have you been a fireman – I mean fire fighter?" Man, I was so nervous to be in the company of such beauty, like when I held Dana for the first time. She was so beautiful and fragile that I had to give her back to her mother for fear that I would drop her.

"Actually, I started a little over a year ago."

"Well, welcome to the 23rd." That's all I could think of to say.

"Thanks. I'm going to work out, but I'll definitely see you later."

"OK, bye." And I waved my hand like Forrest Gump. I felt like a gimp.

I saw Ramsey gawk at her ass when she walked to the bunkroom. When she closed the door, Ramsey and Cap and convulsed with laughter.

"You owe me ten bucks," Cap said to Ramsey.

"I didn't think he would crumble," Ramsey said as he reached in his wallet and pulled out a ten spot.

"We all crumbled around her."

"OK, stop talking like I'm the one who left the room." I turned back to where Naia had gone and scratched my head. "What's up with that?"

"What can I say, the BC bought her in about two weeks ago and things haven't been the same," Cap said and returned to his seat. "Man, I haven't been able to take a decent crap since."

"I'm just glad that I met Tamara before she showed or else I would have been spinning my wheels trying to get her."

"Yeah, and the girl can cook. She feeds us breakfast, lunch and dinner," Cap added.

"Plus, we don't have to fight over who does the dishes. She washes them too."

"That sounds too good to be true." I finally took a seat. I stared at Mark Hayes, the anchor for *Good Day Atlanta*. Something about Naia was familiar.

"What's up Rick?" Ramsey asked.

"Nothing, it's just that Naia reminds me of somebody and I can't quite place it."

"Yeah, like a cross between Garcelle Beauvais and Halle Berry."

"Yeah, maybe that's it." And after that, I shrugged it off and sombered down for the boob tube. No matter what show was on, one of the guys had something to add, whether it was fashion policing or playing name-that-actor.

Somehow it was different, though, without Spoon. I didn't want to bring it up, but I felt bad for his death.

The rest of the day on B shift was uneventful, except for our meals. Naia made pancakes for breakfast, turkey sandwiches for lunch and killer spaghetti with homemade basil sauce for dinner. We were so stuffed that, had there been an alarm, we probably would have fallen asleep at the hose.

Since I completed my investigation of Shana's murder and handed it over to Leicky and Biddings, I needed something to do. In my not-so-distant past, my spare time was juggled between part-time security jobs and – other things. Financially, I didn't need to pick up shifts at Piggly Wiggly, and I had no interest in women. I had a spark for Kimi, but she's not really a woman, she's a reporter.

After I got home, showered and shaved, I called Leicky to get an arrest report on Kennard. I looked forward to seeing his ass fry.

"Homicide, Leicky."

"Detective Leicky." I started, trying to give him props. "This is Rick and I just wanted to check on Kennard's arrest."

I heard hesitation in his voice. "Whoa, you think we can walk up to him and make an arrest?"

"You did with me," I said sarcastically.

"I don't have time for this conversation. What is it that you want?"

"I want you to arrest him, that's what I want."

"Lieutenant Pulliam told us to check his alibi and we did."

"He was there," I hollered into the receiver, sounding desperate. "Isn't that enough?"

"There's no proof that he was in the hospital."

"Proof? What about the pictures I showed you?"

"You want me to take a picture of skull plastered with clay to the DA and say what?" Leicky's was heated. "Rick, I've been in this business a little longer than you and my gut feeling tells me he's not our guy."

"Your original gut told you I was the killer. Maybe your gut is wrong."

"We had a tape of you threatening your wife, and a day later she's dead. Any first-year rookie would look to you first. Comes with the territory."

"Why did he hide from the cameras. Tell me that?"

"The only thing your suspect is guilty of is beating his wife. That wasn't the first time she was there."

"What was his alibi?"

"I can't disclose that information to you." He went silent and I waited him out. "He was at his sister's house, crying on her shoulder."

"His sister's house. How lame is that?"

"It's been verified."

"I'm sure it has."

I had nothing further to say so I simply hung up on him. I threw the phone across the living room floor and paced, heated. One minute I thought my life was settled and the next moment, I'm catapulted back into the tumultuous grind of proving that Kennard was my wife's murderer.

It took me less than five minutes to formulate my plan. First I called Ramsey.

"Hey Ramsey, you working today?"

"Yep, trying to pay for the engagement ring I picked out."

"How much is it?"

"That's kinda personal, don't you think, Rick?"

"Just tell me how much it cost."

The phone went silent as he contemplated an answer. "Thirty-five hundred. Do you think that's too much?" he asked, going from a hardball to a softy.

"Naw, man that's a good price." Now I hesitated. For my plan to work, I needed Ramsey at my beck and call. "Ramsey, something came up with the APD and they are dropping the case against Kennard."

"I thought they would nab him."

"Yeah, me too. But it seems he had an alibi. He was at his sister's house boo-hooing about what he did to Marlene."

"And they bought it?"

"Yeah, they bought it, hook, line and sinker. I need your help proving that he did it."

"How are you going to do that?"

"First, I'm going to buy that engagement ring for you to give to Tamara. Then I'm–"

"Hold on, Rick. What kind of man would I be if I let you buy my girlfriend an engagement ring?"

"Think of it as me hiring you as my partner. I need your help."

"That's a lot of money for help."

"Well, hazard pay is included in the thirty-five hundred."

"Oh shit, you mean hazard pay for going to the Bluff?"

"You got it."

I heard his wheels spinning as he thought about my offer.

"OK, man, I'm in. But only because it's you."

"Great, now what size pants and shirt do you wear?"

"What's that go to do with the price of a kilo in Miami?"

"You'll see. Now just tell me."

When I hung up from Ramsey, I called Kimi to ask for yet another favor. After several rings, the voice-mail system kicked in. I left an urgent message for her to call me as soon as her schedule would allow, giving her my cell phone number. I threw on a plain pair of jeans and the grungiest shirt I could find. Looking for that type of shirt, I now understood why the guys at the 23rd called me Mr. Hollywood. My wardrobe, when viewed from another perspective, was totally designer. But for my new operation, Kenneth Cole was definitely out of the question.

When I found satisfaction in my attire, I headed out, driving down Hairston Road with the radio off. As I gathered my thoughts, I looked around at the leather interior of my Eddie Bauer series Expedition. This was a problem. When I passed a used car lot on Wesley Chapel Road, I slowed down and turned into it.

I circled around the gravel-covered establishment and parked near the office, a mobile home with a five-thousand BTU AC unit sitting on a wood plank outside the front window. A middle-aged white man wearing a pair of beat-up boots met me on the lot. He looked like a retired bull rider from back in the day, red leathery skin, and bow-legged. After I explained what I wanted, I let him sell me an old Pontiac Lemans, 1977 model. I paid seven hundred and fifty dollars cash and tossed in another fifty for the guy to drive the Expedition back to my apartment.

My next stop was the Army surplus store on Ralph McGill Boulevard. I made it there in good time – the Pontiac's eight-cylinder engine raced me there, threatening whiplash from the mach-1 take off. They don't make cars like that anymore. I picked up two pairs of binoculars, canteens and some old Army fatigues for Ramsey and myself. I walked next door to the medical supply store and picked up a used wheelchair.

Next I headed to the office to meet Ramsey. As soon as I found a parking space and began to parallel park, my cell phone rang. It was Kimi.

"You want something from me, don't you?"

"You caught me. The detectives dropped the case and I intend on pursuing it until Kennard fries."

"Kennard? Who is this Kennard?"

I brought her up to speed on the latest developments, with the promise that she'd omit the part about Sheila giving me Marlene's name.

"But I need to know exactly what MARTA department she works in."

"You know that information used to be public, until the transit system's union lobbied against it. The paper doesn't publish those names and salaries anymore."

"Do you think you could look it up in the archives?

"You are going to owe me big time."

"Yes, ma'am."

I ended the call and continued walking to the office. I was fortunate that I didn't terminate the lease, and I stopped in briefly to give a shout out to Doc.

"How you doing, Doc?" I asked, poking my head in the shop.

"If I was doing any better, I'd be the pot of gold at the end of the rainbow."

"Take care, old man." And with that, I eased my head out of the door.

I waited ten minutes before Ramsey showed up. I explained the plan and at first he seemed apprehensive, then with a bit of gentle persuasion, I talked him into it.

He had one other reservation. "What about Kennard? He seen us before. And I don't think he or anybody else could forget two big black dudes like us."

"Trust me on that." I lifted one of the plastic bags from the Army surplus store and handed it to Ramsey. He looked inside and frowned.

"What's this?"

"This is part one to your concern."

He tilted his head, questioning. "How do old Army fatigues solve the recognition problem?"

"When you put them on and we head to the Bluff, you'll see."

We took the Pontiac and drove through downtown until we picked up North Avenue to the Bluff. The closer we got, the better I felt about dropping seven hundred and fifty dollars on the Pontiac, figuring we'd be less likely to get car-jacked in the beat-up car. We parked at a mom-and-pop store at the corner of North and English Avenue. The strategic placement gave us a bird's-eye view of Kennard's house. We used the corner with the convenience store as a catch all for our presence. My reasoning held that people tend to hang out on corners with convenience stores.

The corner store was stripped of any commercial appeal, and papered over with poster-sized advertisements for malt liquor and Newport cigarettes. Ramsey got out and removed from the trunk the wheelchair that I purchased from the medical supply store. Wearing my Army fatigues, a baseball cap and a pair of sunglasses, I slid from the car to the chair and positioned my legs in an awkward stance to give the appearance of a paraplegic.

While Ramsey sat in the car on the passenger side, I rolled into the Korean-owned store and purchased a forty-ounce of Colt 45 to add to my authenticity. The store was small, with three rows for candy, chips and beverages. The tile was worn through to the concrete slab and the shelves looked like they came from the Depression era. When I rolled to the beverage aisle and brought my purchase to the glass-enclosed cashier, I saw a sign posted on the barrier that read, 'Bullets fired at Plexiglas will ricochet'.

When I returned to the car, a scantily clad woman in a skimpy mini skirt that revealed the crease of her buttocks leaned over the passenger side talking to Ramsey. When I rolled up, she gave me a suggestive look, said something to Ramsey and strolled off swaying her tail.

"What's up with that?" I asked Ramsey as I twisted the cap off the beer and crushed the brown sack around the bottle neck.

"I think this may be a ho stroll. She offered her oral services for a small ten-dollar fee."

"That's kind of expensive for a blow job in the Bluff."

"When I declined, she offered me a one-time fifty-percent discount."

"It's a good thing you declined, wouldn't want to mess up tonight's performance with Tamara." I spoke to him while he sat in the car and, while I kept an eye on the Kennard house. We planned it this way, so it would appear to Kennard that we were two drunks shooting the breeze.

"No performance tonight," Ramsey said in a strained voice.

"That time of the month for her?"

"No nothing like that. We decided to wait."

I turned my attention from the Kennard house and looked at him. "You mean to tell me you haven't boned her?" I clenched my fist and moved it in and out in a stroking motion.

He looked the other way and tried to ignore me. After a couple of minutes watching people go in and out of the convenient store, Ramsey turned back to me. "She's a special lady and I ain't none of your damn business if I boned her or not."

That's what I liked so much about Ramsey. Burly as he was, his soft side made up for the natural intimidation.

"C'mon, man, you know I don't have nothing but love for you," I said, taking an imaginary swig from the beer bottle.

We talked in random bouts and we kept an eye on the Kennard house. An hour passed with no hint of activity and we began to get restless. TV stakeouts were more exciting than this and I started to wonder if my plan was worth it. Ramsey wasn't shy about letting me know that he was frying in the hot car. I suggested that he turn on the radio to get his mind off the heat. When he reached over to turn it on, we heard a series of gun shots coming from the direction of the Kennard house.

Suddenly a slender man dressed in dirty clothes bolted from the house across the street from Kennard's house. He had a brown paper bag in his hand and I could tell that his unkempt afro hadn't seen a barber in years. We watched as he struggled to keep up his pace, when someone else emerged from the same house. The second man clutched his chest with one hand and a gun with the other. When he turned in the direction of the running man, he fired five shots, missing the runner each time. I looked at Ramsey in disbelief as no one in the neighborhood stopped doing what they were doing.

"Maybe we should cut out before the police get here?" I asked Ramsey, not wanting to stick around for questioning.

"I was thinking the same thing."

We executed our egress plan, which called for Ramsey to place the wheelchair in the trunk when I slid out of it. When I started the car and put it in gear, I caught a glimpse of Kennard leaving his house. He wore a jacket despite the scorching heat and looked over his shoulder as he walked toward us. I sat behind the steering wheel, not knowing whether to take or tail him.

I looked at Ramsey and he signaled to me the go-ahead with the tail. When Shana's killer walked past us, the adrenaline rushed through my veins as my entire body tensed up for an attack. Homicidal thoughts ran rampant in my head as he crossed by the car. I held on to the steering wheel to stop myself from rushing him. Ramsey must have seen my white knuckles gripping the steering wheel.

"Chill out, Rick. He'll eventually show his true colors."

Just as I was about to respond to Ramsey, Kennard ducked into the convenience store, making one final glance behind him.

"Ramsey, I know he's the one, I can feel it in my bones."

Ramsey sighed, and we waited for Kennard to finish in the store. "Just what are you expecting to accomplish with this surveillance?"

"If I can get proof that he's a murderer, then the APD will reopen the investigation and arrest him. All we have to do is wait till he fucks up."

"What makes you so sure that he will kill again? Maybe he just wanted to stop his punching-bag of a wife from seeing Shana."

I loosened my grip on the steering wheel and turned to Ramsey. "What else do I do, sit at home and watch TV. Let's just see what turns up, OK?" I turned away and watched the store. "Beats waiting on the police to pull their thumb out of their asses."

A Buick pulled up to the curb, parallel to the store. I saw Kennard get in the passenger seat and the car turned left onto North Avenue.

I immediately followed them, keeping a safe distance. When the driver of the Buick, another white man smoking a cigarette, turned right on Northside Drive, I had no idea where they were going, but Ramsey kept an eye on them while I drove.

I did notice that Kennard kept his head down, like he was counting change, and frequently looking up when the driver slowed down or made stops. When we passed Turner Field, we kept driving until we reached Grant Park. The Buick stopped in one of the park's many lots alongside the rolling grass area. I picked a spot off Boulevard to park and observe. Kennard still had his head down, but now the driver watched him intently. It made me curious to what they were staring at. When Kennard's head rolled back on the headrest, I knew they were shooting dope. Kennard had been cooking up the heroin while the driver made his way to the park. I wondered why they would chance shooting up in the park instead of the comfort of home.

A few moments had passed with no action. Both Kennard's and the driver's head lay back on the headrests. I looked over at Ramsey and whispered, "How long does the high last?"

"Why are you whispering?" he said.

"Because I don't want them to hear us."

"Rick, we are nearly a quarter of a mile away from them," Ramsey belted. "And no, I don't know how long a heroin buzz lasts."

"You don't have to holler, I'm not a quarter mile away." I reached into the backseat and pulled out my binoculars from the Army surplus store. When I got a closer look at the two men in the old Buick, I noticed that their eyelids were partially closed, revealing the whites of their eyes. It made me wonder what kind of drug had the power to make someone's eyes roll to the back of his head.

A dog came into view near the car and began sniffing on the ground. He was the muttiest, homeliest and ugliest dog I had ever seen in my life. The mutt got closer to the car and paused. He was on the passenger side when he jumped up and started licking Kennard on the face. My heart dropped at the site of this homeless dog giving out affection at the first chance it got. Still peering through the binoculars, I saw Kennard stumble out of his drug-induced stupor. He blinked, disoriented, and when he saw the likes of the mutt licking him, Kennard jumped out of the car and began kicking the dog in the chest area with his old cowboy boots. From where Ramsey and me sat, we could hear high-pitched yelps coming from the dog. Kennard kept kicking him and the pain I felt for that mutt at that moment was unbearable. I wanted to run from the safety of my seat and take that dog's place, making it a fair fight. Then the dog got quiet and stopped moving. Kennard kept kicking him. Other people had stopped what they were doing and watched the horror of the scene.

When Kennard saw that he had an audience, he stopped, got back in the Buick and the two men took off, throwing divots of gravel in the air as they sped off. My heart raced as I saw the listless body of the dog lying on the ground. I caught glimpses of his chest area rising and falling in what appeared to be strained attempts at breathing. When I glanced around and saw that the other people were going about their business, I jumped out of the car and raced to where the dog lay. As I ran, I felt heat boil in my chest, as I hadn't worked out since the fire at the Briarcliff Summit. Plus, I felt the strain from the Percocet slow me down. I forced myself to ignore the pain.

When I reached the dog, he held his head down, breathing hard. I was about to give up on him when he strained to look up at me. When I saw those sad, hurt eyes and I remembered the affection that he freely gave to Kennard, I bent down and gently scooped him up.

"Come on, boy, I'm going to take care of you."

I jogged back to the Pontiac, not wanting to hurt him any more than he had already sustained. When I reached the car, Ramsey was in the driver's seat, ready to go.

"Where to?" he asked. I felt a wave of relief that he supported my decision, instead of being condescending.

"I saw a vet's office across from Dugan's."

And with that, Ramsey took off, not saying another word. I looked down at the poor, homeless dog and saw his rib cage showing through his coat. The poor animal probably lived his entire life scrounging for food and love. At that moment, I felt the pressure build up in my eye sockets as tears filled them.

We reached the Banfield Pet Hospital in ten minutes and I noticed that the mutt's breathing was more labored. As soon as I entered the facility, the receptionist at the front desk immediately came around to where I stood. She had a warm and gentle aura as she took a look at the dog and felt for a pulse.

"What happened?" she asked, with a guarded look.

"We saw a man beating this dog in Grant Park."

I saw her immediately relax. "Bring him back," she said as she led the way to the patient room. "Does he have a name?"

"No, this is my first day meeting him."

When I laid his body on the metal table, the dog gave me a please-don't-leave-me look. My heart sank. "I'm not going anywhere, boy, just get yourself well."

The receptionist led me out as she called for the doctor. I sat in the lobby and waited. Ramsey sat with me and not once did he seem impatient. I paced the floor, while looking periodically to the closed door. I felt like an expectant father waiting for the news of a newborn baby.

It was thirty minutes before someone came out to talk with me. He was a white man wearing a white lab coat and I suspected he was the doctor.

"Are you the owner of the dog?"

I knew he wanted to say ugly dog. "No, I'm not the owner, I think he's homeless."

"What happened?"

"We saw a man beating the shit out of him and we brought him here. Is he going to be all right?"

"Well, normally I don't recommend this, but since you aren't his owner, I would suggest euthanasia."

"You mean putting him to sleep?"

"Unfortunately, yes. We x-rayed him and he has two broken ribs and a punctured lung. The cost to save him would be roughly about seven thousand dollars for the surgery."

I studied the doctor with a look of disbelief. My first reaction was to go along with the recommendation of euthanasia. But the more I thought about it, the more I couldn't bear the thought of the dog dying with final memories of someone that he was trying to love kicking him to death.

"Doctor, do whatever you need to do to save him. Whatever it takes."

The doctor tilted his head and looked at me with an expression somewhere between disbelief and fondness.

I filled out the necessary paperwork and was told that the dog would need to stay two days after the surgery for observations. I was amazed that they treated animals with the same care as humans. I left all my contact numbers, and we left Banfield Pet Hospital feeling good.

15

After a fretful sleep, I woke the next morning thinking of the dog. I made a cup of coffee and tried to occupy my mind with other things. I made a sausage, egg and cheese sandwich and wished I had some grits to go along with it. When I took my plate to the sink, I noticed the laptop from Shana's office. I retrieved the computer and turned it on to see if I could find any additional information on Marlene. While it was booting, I still thought of the dog, so I decided to call the vet to check his status.

"My name is Rick Edison and I dropped–"

"Yes, Mr. Edison, the dog is doing well." I recognized the voice as the receptionist's. "He's stable now, but we need to keep him for a couple more days."

I felt a huge smile grow on my face. "Thank you for taking care of him."

"No, thank you for caring. We are rooting for him." She paused. "Mr. Edison, you need to start thinking of a name for your new dog."

After I hung up, it occurred to me that I was going to be a pet owner. I dreaded the thought of taking him to the humane society where I was certain no one would choose an old, ugly mutt. The ring of the telephone disrupted my thoughts. "Rick, this is Kimi."

I don't know about the Age of Aquarius or cosmic forces, but whatever twist of luck that brought her into my life during the worst time in my life was a force I was pleased with. The subtle everything's-gonna-be-all-right calmness that she made me feel was always welcomed. "Hello stranger."

"Stranger? You just spoke to me yesterday."

Again, she caught me letting out one of those idiotic phrases. "I was just making sure you were on your toes."

"Rick, if I didn't know better, I'd say you were full of shit."

"Such language for such a beautiful lady."

"I went to an all-girl Catholic school."

"Oh, I'm sorry to hear that."

We both let out a laugh and it felt good that I could carry on somewhat of a normal conversation with Kimi without murder being the topic of conversation.

"I have some information for you, and I actually learned something from my research."

"Is that right?"

"Remember when I told you that MARTA used to publish employee information annually in the AJC?"

"Yes."

"Well, I learned that in order to satisfy grievances from the union, MARTA had to publish their annual records somewhere, as long as it was not in the newspaper where the neighbors could see how much the employees next door made the previous year."

"I can understand that."

"Guess where they publish this information?"

"Um, the library." I just threw something out so she would tell me.

"No, on their website. Can you believe that?" I heard a tone of excitement in Kimi's voice. She genuinely liked doing research.

"So all I have to do is type in www.marta.com and what?"

"Actually the URL is www.itsmarta.com. It appears that a Hispanic gentleman purchased the domain name marta.com in adoration of his beloved wife Marta."

"Oh." That was all I could think to respond to that trivial piece of information she shared.

"Your girl is a clerk in the Avondale rail maintenance center," she said.

"Kimi, you are the greatest."

"Tell me something I don't already know."

Before we hung up the phone, I promised her a dinner at Atlanta's premier steak house, Bones, when Kennard was behind bars.

I swung into action, showering, shaving and dressing for the visit the Avondale rail maintenance center. I decided to take the low rider because it reminded me of my youth, when a '77 Pontiac was a cool car, and I liked the way it ran.

I knew exactly where the maintenance line was because when I attended Atlanta Metropolitan College, I rode the subway to and from school and work. Even though I had meager funds and no transportation, that was the best time in my life. It was a time when I appreciated a ride to school or a lift home from my minimum-wage fast food job.

The Avondale Rail Maintenance Center was located in the suburb of Avondale Estates, a city annexed by rich white citizens from Decatur, which at the time was well on its way to becoming a black majority suburb. City officials kept the Memorial Drive entrance blocked, so that anyone wanting to cross its precious city line had to first pass the city's police department, who were only too happy to stop a suspicious-looking person for questioning. Suspicious being the color of one's skin.

I took College Avenue and swung on Arcadia. This led me to the maintenance center's parking lot. Inside, I parked in front of the only office type of building I saw, and entered. It was a one-story building surrounded by a field of old MARTA rail cars, and reminded me of a rail car junkyard. Inside at the front desk, I saw a woman that I instinctively knew was Marlene Kennard. She was dumpy-looking, with stringy brown hair and droopy shoulders. She wore no makeup, not that it would've done her much good.

She looked up from her computer monitor.

"Can I help you?"

"Marlene Kennard?"

"Yes, how may I help you?"

At this point, I had no idea what to say to her. What do you say to the wife of a killer? I could have knocked myself in the head for not thinking of an angle. But to my surprise, the chains and wheels in my brain kicked in, and amazingly, something came to mind.

"My name's Graham Fisher from Emory Clinic." I said in a voice more polished and proper than my ordinary one. I had heard Shana go from a lazy Ebonics to a crisp Caucasian dialect, and never before had I envied the ability. "As a designated representative from the Clinic, we are visiting all of Dr. Edison's patients in hopes of securing referrals to other psychologists."

She clutched her sweater around her chest like she was shutting off any intrusion to her insides. "Why, won't Dr. Edison be coming back?"

My heart skipped a beat. "Mrs. Kennard, what have you heard?"

"When I went to my appointment," she said, looking from side to side, "they told me she wasn't available, indefinitely." She leaned in closer to me from the other side of the front desk. "Did she have to leave town?"

"I'm sorry, but Dr. Edison is dead."

She took one gulp and clutched her chest. It was something about her chest that she was protecting and I didn't know what. After a few unspoken moments, her eyes fixed wildly on me. She then leaned forward and started rocking back and forth in sort of an upright fetal position. I don't know the medical symptoms of catatonic schizophrenia, but I'd be willing to bet that if I looked it up on the Internet, she would be exhibiting signs of that disorder.

"Mrs. Kennard, I'd like to set you up with some counseling."

"Oh, I won't be able to talk to nobody else." She looked up from her rocking.

"Well, as a member of the staff, I'd like to ask you about your husband."

"What does he have to do with anything?" she asked suddenly.

"Well, um you see, we just want to make sure you are OK." That was all I could think of to say, and I could hear in my voice that I was losing credibility fast.

"If you don't have anything further, I'd like you to leave now." She turned to her monitor, trying to push me out.

"Has he been beating you lately?" I have no idea where that came from but as soon as I said it, the blood drained from her face and made her white skin appear somewhat translucent.

"I don't know what you are talking about." Her voice grew louder. "He wouldn't hurt a flea."

He wouldn't hurt a flea, but he'll beat the shit out of the flea's benefactor.

"It's just that since Jimmy got laid off, he's been feeling like he doesn't contribute enough."

"Marlene, you have to get away from him, Jimmy is a dangerous man."

She looked at me quizzically. "Who are you anyway?"

I guess my attempt at being Emory staff had failed. I just needed to save this poor woman somehow but I wasn't equipped to do that. Had she been trapped in a fire, I had special training for that. Then, something made me pause as I felt a strange sensation. It was a little voice inside my head saying something that I couldn't make out, but it made the hairs on the back of my neck stand up.

"Listen, I am Dr. Edison's husband. I have reason to believe that Jimmy, your husband, may have killed her to stop you from seeing her."

"That's crazy. Jimmy just wants the best for me. He loves me."

"Do you know about his drug usage?"

"Jimmy would never do drugs. You have the wrong man. Now please leave me alone."

At least I knew why Kennard went to the park to shoot up. He didn't want his wife coming home from work catching him with a needle in his arm and drug paraphernalia scattered in the den.

When I drove away from the rail yard, I realized that any help from the wife would be futile. She was dead set on defending that lowlife, snake in the grass husband of hers. She was in complete denial. I had no other avenues to check, and since this was the last day of my two-day break, I decided to hang out in the Bluff to see what else I could find out on Jimmy Kennard.

When I got to the convenience store, I realized that I didn't have my wheelman to get the wheelchair out of the trunk. And I thought that a paraplegic going into the trunk to retrieve his own wheelchair wouldn't sit well, even with the people in the Bluff. I decided to go to the gas station on Ashby Street and pay someone to get the chair out of the trunk.

I parked at the Happy Store self-service station with a large sign requesting payment up front for gasoline. Two men and a woman stood in front of the building, checking me out. When I motioned one of the men over to the car, he obliged and immediately asked what I wanted, heroin or crack. I told him neither but I'd pay five bucks if he'd get the wheelchair out of the trunk.

I didn't mind leaving the Pontiac parked at the Happy Store-the last time I checked, there was no black market for a 1977 Pontiac. I rolled down Ashby in the wheelchair until I reached English Avenue, passing Kennard's house en route to the corner.

When I passed the house, I noticed a privacy fence in the backyard with a chain and lock at the entry gate. Satisfied that I could see the house's only exit from the corner, I rolled on. When I reached my corner, I went in the store for a forty-ounce of beer, and came out pretending to drink it. This time I saw a couple of dudes hanging out on the side of the store directly across from where I parked the wheelchair.

I sat for hours watching the Kennard house without incident. I was bored and getting hungry when my cell phone rang. It was Lisa from the CDC. I had forgotten about her.

"Got some good news and some bad news."

"Give it to me."

I heard papers shuffling. "I ran a sampling of agents found in the talcum powder found in her rectum to verify its origin. Sometimes we can pinpoint a particular chemical to a specific region."

I wished she'd just tell me instead of giving me the whole back-story.

"My findings were inconclusive of the results from the tox screen."

"Is that the good news or the bad news?" I asked.

"Neither. Your medical examiner's talcum powder was dried dye residue from a Coca-Cola bottle."

I wanted to jump out of the wheelchair. "How did a Coca-Cola bottle get in her–" The word would not escape my lips.

"That's the good news."

"That's good news?"

"She wasn't sodomized."

I saw a MARTA bus stop at the corner across from where I sat. To my consternation, Marlene Kennard emerged and headed toward her house. I thought it ironic that not only did she work for MARTA, but she rode it too. "How did a Coke bottom get up there?"

"That's the bad news. I have no idea." She covered the receiver as she talked to someone else. "But, I was able to confirm the other findings in the report." I heard a loud noise in the background.

I waited for her to finish.

"Listen Rick, I gotta go. Thanks for the purse." She hung up.

Yeah, thanks for nothing. I said to myself.

A feeling of confusion took over. My mind wanted to believe that she was sodomized because it was hard to understand why Kennard rammed a coke bottle up her. It made no sense. I tried to get into his small mind to figure out why he did that. Then my attention turned to the Kennard house. After Marlene entered, Kennard left. He walked in the opposite direction to where I sat. I moved quickly, wheeling the chair in his direction, trying to keep up, but my shoulder began hurting and I slowed down, losing sight of him when he turned the corner.

Damn!

Since I was close to the Happy Store, I decided to leave for the day and chalk it up as a day in the life of a detective. No foul, no flag.

The next day when I reported for work on B shift, the usual suspects were there, including Ms. Naia. Cap was gone on a scheduled off day. I took a seat at the table with the rest of the guys, waiting on breakfast. Naia busied herself at the stove, whipping up eggs, grits, bacon and sausage. I don't know if it was the anticipation of a great meal or the view of her backside that kept us there, but either way we were pretty much guaranteed satisfaction.

She served our individual plates and to my surprise, she made mine first. I began eating as she dished up JT's plate. When I looked up to thank her, I noticed that she was wearing another long-sleeved shirt. It was July in Atlanta. I pushed the oddity to the back of my mind because my grits and eggs were so damn good. When Naia finished serving our breakfast, she excused herself from the kitchen. Ramsey looked up.

"You aren't going to eat?"

"No, you help yourself to more, I have to go work out."

"You look fine to me," Ramsey said with a mouth full of buttered toast.

"If I don't watch my shape, nobody else will." I couldn't tell if it was my imagination, but I could have sworn that she brushed her breast against my back when she walked past me.

Smelly confirmed what I was thinking. "Man, that sister has got the meltdown for you."

"Did you see that?" I asked, being careful not to raise my voice.

"We saw it, all right. She made your plate first and she even asked about you the other day."

"What do you mean she asked about me the other day?"

I turned to Smelly, waiting for an answer, when my cell phone rang. It was Teri Van Hart.

"I need to tell you something."

I got up from the table and walked into the engine room. "Go on."

"I ran some more inclusive test on what I thought was talcum powder residue in the crevices of the sphincter muscles–"

"It's dried up dye."

"How did you know that?" she asked, probing.

I remained silent.

"I need to see you in person."

"I'm on duty today. I can come to your office tomorrow, first thing."

"No! Not here. What time do you get off? Maybe we can meet at a bar."

"I'm a fire fighter, we work twenty-four-hour shifts."

"Ooh, that's right. I'm sorry."

I heard her heavy breathing over the line and a ripple of fear washed over me.

"Well, can I at least come to the station and explain it to you?"

I agreed to let her come. The guys at fire stations all across the country had female visitors from time to time. Sometimes, even their kids showed up wanting a handout or something. After I gave her driving directions, we agreed on seven that evening.

When Van Hart arrived at the station, she insisted we sit in her car instead of at the kitchen table. I agreed until I saw that her mode of transportation was a Hyundai Sonata. I surmised it was the student loans that prevented the BMW.

"Do you mind if we sit in the Expedition?" I said, pointing to my legs. "You know, my long legs and all."

When we got in the car, I turned the ignition so that we could enjoy AC. I saw someone peeking through the blinds and thought of Ramsey. Van Hart seemed edgy. "Please tell me what's going on?"

"First tell me how you knew it was dye and not talcum powder like I first reported?"

"I got a copy of the police report with the tox screen in it."

She turned to face me. "So you stole the report?"

I sank down. "Something like that."

She gazed out the windshield while she collected her thoughts. "That's called obstruction of justice."

"Please don't tell Leicky. It's just that–"

"Never mind. You may have done the case a favor."

"How's that?"

"When Leicky came to the morgue a few days ago, he needed a copy of the tox screen to include in the new file. Then the crime scene guys came by with a second set of blood samples from the Dumpster, again, for the new file. I had my file out and the new samples." She lowered her head. "Rick, I made a terrible mistake assuming that the powdery substance was talcum."

"At least we know. But why did he use a coke bottle?"

"That's just it. It wasn't a he, it was a woman."

My chest constricted and I literally couldn't breathe. I gasped for air and pounded my chest until I felt my lungs loosen up.

"What are you telling me?" I asked, voice tighter than I wanted it to be.

"It means your wife's killer may not have been a man."

"But I know who the killer is," I said, staring at the steering wheel. "It's Jimmy Kennard."

"You were able to ID the craniofacial reconstruction?"

Everything was happening so fast, I had forgotten to tell her. After I explained the events that unfolded with Marlene and the file and the subsequent visit to her house, Van Hart looked worried.

"What's wrong?"

"Rick, I am so sorry but I will need your permission to exhume your wife's body so we can do more tests with the latest piece of information we got."

"You mean you want to dig up her body from the grave and poke around her some more?"

She looked down, avoiding eye contact. "Yes, unfortunately, that's what that means."

I took a deep breath, remembering what my grandmother told me years ago. She told me to take deep breaths when I felt angry and for the first time, I finally listened. "Teri, why is exhuming her body the only option? Can't she rest in peace?" After the words left my mouth, I realized that I sounded like a tired cliché, but at this point in my life, I no longer cared about coining a trendy hip-hop phrase.

"Rick, this is totally my fault for making such an elementary assumption. Believe me, it took a lot for me to come to you with this."

My body wanted to yell, 'Hell no,' but something in my mind wanted to oblige. I took the middle ground. "Can I think about it for a few days?"

She looked out the window, disappointment showing in her body language, "I guess that's better than a no."

She opened the door and stepped down. Before she swung it closed, she gave me her last pitch. “Rick, I wouldn’t do anything with the Kennard guy until I can run some more tests.”

After Van Hart left the station, I went to the bunkroom and lay on my bed. As I gazed down and saw my duffel bag, thoughts of swallowing a handful of Percocet crossed my mind. I wanted to journey to the land of oblivion and take my time coming back, but I had a job to do. I forced myself not to think about the unspeakable decision I had to make. As I dozed off, I had a dream that someone was watching me.

16

I slept through the night and woke up ravenous. I dashed home and changed into my Army fatigues, then I headed to the Bluff. There, I planned to continue the stakeout, hoping to find some tangible evidence against Kennard. I just couldn't believe that a woman was capable of such a brutal murder as Van Hart thought.

Instead of enjoying a sit-down breakfast at the Waffle King restaurant, I called in for take-out. I raced through the wavering traffic in the Pontiac, trying to get there before Kennard left the house. Despite my mind-set, the day was turning out to be one of those clear sunny days with skies as blue as the Caribbean Sea. My cell phone rang.

"Mr. Edison, this is Jackie from Banfield pet hospital."

I immediately thought the worst. "How is he doing?"

"He's great. And I'll tell you, he has an appetite."

"I'm on my way."

I looked at the food sitting on the seat next to me and decided that it wasn't enough. I stopped by a fast food joint and picked up a half dozen chicken and steak breakfast biscuits. I caught myself feeling excited about the dog.

When I got there, I saw that the pet hospital had given him the run of the house. He moved slowly and deliberately, but he was moving, and that was the most important thing. I paid the whopping bill and to my surprise, I felt hopeful. The dog followed me to the car and immediately jumped in the front seat next to the food. His little tail wagged feverishly as he sniffed the contents. I had intentions of waiting until I got to the Bluff before I fed him, but I couldn't resist the temptation of giving it to him now.

"OK, fellow, let's have at it." I opened one of the chicken biscuits and placed it on the seat. He nosed the meat away from the biscuit and wolfed down the piece of chicken. After he finished, he turned to me and out of the blue, licked my face with enough slobber and chewed-up pieces of meat to make me want to puke. But I didn't have the heart to stop him.

"I guess I have to give you a name, uh buddy?" He let out a bark as if he were responding to me. I had to smile despite his awful looks. "How about

Ugmo? 'Cause you are the ugliest dog I've seen." He let out a whimper. "OK, maybe that's a little cruel."

When I unwrapped a steak biscuit and watched him wolf it down again, I decided on a name. "OK, Scruffy, how 'bout that?" And he barked again. "Then it's settled."

Now that I had a partner, I had to make one more stop before my surveillance of Kennard's place. I took I-285 to LaVista and went to the PetSmart supermarket for dog supplies. By the time I left, I had purchased nearly two hundred dollars worth of dog food, treats, bones and anything I could think of to make Scruffy's life enjoyable.

I parked at the Happy Store again and paid another man to help me with my wheelchair. I placed the collar and leash on Scruffy and we rolled down Kennard's street toward the corner store.

For nearly an hour, I sat in the wheelchair on the corner and nothing unusual happened at the Kennard house. I made it there around ten that morning and I guessed it was close to lunchtime. I wondered if he had left the house before I got there, and I decided to call and find out but I needed his telephone number. I pulled out my cell phone, hoping it wouldn't blow my cover as a poor paraplegic.

Aisha answered on the second ring.

"What, no meetings today?"

"Shut up, Ricky, you know I work from home."

"I need a huge favor from you, my most beautiful sister."

"I'm your only sister, but I'll take that compliment."

"If I give you a name, can you get me a telephone number?"

"You want me to access company records for your personal use?"

"Yeah, sort of."

"I have a good thing with BellSouth and you want me to jeopardize it so you can get in some lady's panties."

"I don't chase women anymore. Why is that so hard for people to believe?"

"Um, for starters, your track record. You can take a man out of the bush, but you can't take the bush out of the man."

"My, aren't we the queen of comedy this afternoon. I really need a number. Please?" I groveled for her sake. I had to play on her sympathy, and groveling usually did the trick. In fact, she and my grandmother were the only two women whom I ever had to beg.

"What's the name?" she asked dejectedly.

"Marlene or Jimmy Kennard. That's K-E-N-N-A–"

"I know how to spell Kennard. Hold on while I check."

Normally I would return the smart-ass remark, but I decided to be cool and let her have the upper hand. I thought I would hear the pounding of the keyboard, but instead I just heard paper shuffling. She came back to the phone.

"I have a Marlene Kennard at 135 English Avenue."

"Yes, that's the one."

"Please hold for the number," she said in the 411 lady's tone.

"Hahaha, you are so funny."

She shuffled some more papers. "For your information, the number's published in the telephone book," she said, then read the number off to me.

"Well, if that's the case, I don't have to give you that Coach purse that I was going to give you as a thank-you present."

"I have two words for you. Navy Blue." And she hung up.

Scruffy sat on the sidewalk next to my chair like we had been together since his birth. I turned from him and called the number Aisha had given me. After the third ring, Kennard answered the phone in a raspy voice. I simply hit the End key on my cell phone and hung up on him.

Satisfied that he was there, I was content that I had not missed him. As time passed, I grew weary of the monotony. Scruffy gave me as much attention as he could, being that he just had major surgery. I had the weirdest notion to order a pizza for delivery, but shunned the idea knowing that Papa John's wouldn't deliver to the Bluff.

I saw Ramsey's mini-skirt, discounted hooker. She came up to me and asked me to buy her a pack of Newport cigarettes. Out of loneliness for some human interaction, I gave her five bucks and told her to bring me back the change. She took my money and dissappeared.

Sometime in the late afternoon, a black man came and visited with me. He rattled on about his brother being in the Army and how he intended on opening up a 'bidness,' as he called it. He had grand plans to one day become a millionaire, and mentioned that he had that special 'bidness' sense. All I could do was encourage him, because anything I may have suggested would have come across like I was some kind of pretentious wanna-be. But maybe not, since I was suppose to be a washed-out, crippled veteran. He continued to stand there and talk to me until he saw one of his cronies walk down the street. He strode at a clip until he caught up with him, leaving me alone again. The terrible feeling of boredom came back, and for the life of me I could not understand how someone could do this every day. Marlene Kennard eventually came home, and I geared up, ready to roll at the notion that Kennard might come out, but he didn't. He stayed in for the entire evening.

Before dusk, I headed around the corner and called it quits for the day. When I got to the gas station, I found the back window of the Pontiac in pieces on the backseat. When I rolled closer, I saw that all the dog food and accessories were gone. In disgust, I took off for home, not caring who saw me put the wheelchair in the trunk and walk to the driver's side. I had to make another stop at the PetSmart, but I didn't get nearly the amount of goodies I got earlier.

When Scruffy and I made it back to the apartment, out of frustration, I took a drink of the leftover tequila. With the air-conditioning humming and Scruffy relaxing, I felt the warm comfort of the liquor enter my bloodstream. It was a relief. I wanted to forget the pain and the emptiness that had sunk in, but all I could think about was that I had no one to go home to and no one to love. I understood what drove people to take mind-altering drugs, to simply escape from their selves. Instead of shooting drugs into my veins, though, I opted for the slower path of pouring tequila down my throat. The more I drank, the more depressed I got.

I needed to shake off the self-pity that grew inside me. I tried to get off the couch, but it held me like glue to fabric. I wanted to call Dana to say hello, but I couldn't move my arm far enough to pick up the phone. All I had strength to do was to pour another drink. And another one, until I passed out.

17

I was jolted out of a deep slumber from a pounding noise. I didn't know if it was the throbbing of my head, but when I opened my eyes, I had a sense of déjà vu and heard the knock at the door followed by Scruffy's bark. I got up off the couch and felt a sharp pain in my head that came from drinking too much tequila. I reached the door, peered out and saw Ramsey on the other side. I let him in and walked back to the couch.

"You ready to hit the trail?" he asked as I tried to get comfortable. When I finally settled in, I saw Scruffy by the door, pouting.

Shit, I have to let the dog out.

I got back up, attached his leash. "Be right back."

Scruffy walked me to wherever he wanted to handle his business, and to my embarrassment, he decided to release himself in one of Post Apartment's tulip beds. I smiled in spite of my mammoth hangover. When was I ever going to learn to leave tequila alone? One thing I did realize, the hangover got my mind off my other problems.

After Scruffy fertilized the tulips, we headed back. When we made it to the breezeway I heard tires screeching, and when I turned to check it out, I saw none other than Leicky and Biddings coming around the curve in their Crown Victoria. I sighed and kept walking. They followed me into the apartment.

"Come on in, why don't you," I said bitterly.

Ramsey had a puzzled looked on his face.

"Leicky and Biddings, you remember Willie Ramsey."

Ramsey nodded. Leicky helped himself to a seat on the couch. I sat on the chair, resting my elbows on my lap and waited.

"Rick, we have expedited your ex-wife's murder case," Leicky led in. "And we'd like you to come to the station."

I looked up, "What, am I under arrest again?" Somehow I didn't care anymore.

This time Biddings spoke up. "Actually, we need your help. Unless we find a strong suspect, we have to turn this over to the Feds."

"Why the FBI?" Ramsey asked.

I looked at Biddings, then Leicky. "What's with this new sense of urgency?"

This time Leicky lowered his head. "Another doctor has been murdered."

It was always strange to hear others refer to Shana as a doctor. Somehow, I still saw her as that fine young thing that I met back in '82.

"What does that have to do with me?"

"Why don't we go to the station and we'll explain it there." He looked at Ramsey.

"Whatever you have to tell me, you can say in front of him."

Leicky shot me a look of disgust but then I saw him correct himself. He paused. "The murder had the same MO as your wife's."

I cocked my head as I had seen Scruffy do. "MO?"

"Modus operandi or method of operation. It's the criminal's behavior pattern for the means of attack."

"Some people call it the killer's trademark." Biddings added.

Leicky continued. "Dr. Van Hart's body was found in the morgue with her eyes bludgeoned out."

I didn't hear any other words after he said 'Dr. Van Hart.' My heart sank and fear took over from there. "I just saw her the other– How can she be dead?"

"That's right, you knew her. I forgot, she stitched your wrist when you rammed it through the viewing glass at the morgue," Leicky said and grabbed his notepad and began writing something. "Undoubtedly the perp made his way in, killed Van Hart, and set her body up in the cooler to make it look like a regular stiff."

"What were you two doing together?" Biddings asked.

It was a simple enough question. "She informed me that some test had come back that led her to believe that the killer could be a woman."

"Damn, I should've gotten that report from DIES." Leicky stood up walked to the window.

"I told her you all but dropped the case. Maybe since I was the only one actively pursuing the killer, she told me."

Leicky paced the living room. For the first time I saw that he was actually mad. "Had I gotten that information, I might have been able to save her life. Now, because of your interference, another woman is dead."

I didn't like the sound of those accusations and my first reaction was to jump to the defensive, but that didn't solve anything previously and wasn't looking good for me now.

"What can I do to help?"

"Tell us exactly what she told you."

I reminded them about the craniofacial ID that Van Hart had sculpted and the recognition of Kennard. Biddings was the first one to see the flag.

"How did you make this Kennard out?"

"Um – Shana was visiting his wife in the hospital and I just paid her a visit and Kennard answered the door." I felt the words stumble out of my mouth like a kindergartner trying to make a complete and coherent sentence. I secretly hoped that they didn't pick up on my stammering.

"Back up," Leicky said, as I saw his eyes focusing on me. He had caught on to my hem and haw. "How did you get Dr. Van Hart to do the craniofacial sculpting?"

I sighed a breath of relief.

"Go on."

"Well, Teri– I mean Dr. Van Hart, knew I was looking for a man because she molded him." I caught a glimpse of Biddings give Leicky a guarded look. "So when she got the test results back from the lab in Phoenix, she wanted to warn me that I was looking at the wrong guy."

"What specifically did she say about the test results?"

When he asked that question, I vividly remembered sitting in the Expedition with her just the other day. I couldn't believe she was dead. "She told me that, in error, she assumed the substance in Shana's um–"

I couldn't let those words exit my mouth. Scruffy must have sensed something because he came over and sat next to me.

"Just tell us what the substance was," Leicky said gently.

"It was dried-up dye from a Coca-Cola bottle." I saw the looked of shock on their faces, including Ramsey's. Then Leicky began flipping through his notebook, not writing but searching for something.

"They found some kind of powdery substance in Van Hart's rectum, too. But what does that have to do with the killer being a woman?"

"I'm sorry, but you see, I didn't have luxury of asking leading questions because I didn't know what to ask." I raised my voice. He didn't have to say that word and he knew it.

"Did she say anything else?" Biddings asked.

It was a chore to think. I had a terrible hangover from drinking too much tequila and Van Hart was murdered. Something bothered me about the two deaths. They seemed too related, not just by the MO but something else – and I couldn't pin-point it. I remembered the great meal we shared at Morton's Steakhouse and her exuberance about her sculpture of Kennard. Thinking back, she played a big role in my life after Shana's death, beginning with stitching my wrist. "She asked if she could exhume Shana's body and run more tests."

"What!" Leicky hurled himself off the couch and made his way to my telephone. I was surprised when he turned and asked if he could use it.

After Leicky hung up, he sat back down. "Looks like the Feds will be joining our investigation," he said to Biddings.

"Sharon ran Van Hart's murder through HEAT?"

"You got it."

"Shit," Biddings let out and adjusted his tie.

I had no idea of what they were talking about, but I intended to find out. "What is this HEAT you're talking about?"

"That's our Homicide Evaluation and Assessment Tracking. It has a real-time link to the FBI's ViCAP." Leicky looked at me and realized he did it again. "Violent Criminal Apprehension Program."

"Did you enter Shana's file in the HEAT system?"

"Standard operating procedure."

"Then why is the FBI jumping in on Dr. Van Hart's murder case and not Shana's?"

"ViCAP's automated link picks up on two or more cases with the same MO."

"In other words, a serial killer."

"So to speak."

It was hard for me to grasp that Shana's death was a random act of violence. For some awful reason, knowing or thinking that Kennard had killed her made it more acceptable, if that's possible. But a random murder was harder to come to terms with. "So what's the next step?"

"We need you to come down to the precinct and tell us everything you know."

"Now you want my help?"

The room was quiet.

Leicky got up and gazed out of the window. "I thought you killed your ex-wife. For the money and custody." He hesitated. "Now we'll probably get our asses chewed for fucking up."

"So now that your ass is in a sling, you want my help? You can forget about–"

"Yo, Rick, why don't you hear them out," Ramsey interrupted me and for a split second, all heads turned to him. "You said it yourself that the police had more resources than you."

He made sense, even though my pride wanted me to say no. But I had to brush my pride aside because the only thing that mattered was sitting behind the glass walls when they pulled the switch to fry the bastard that killed Shana. I looked at Scruffy, who sat there oblivious to the tension in the room.

"Why can't we talk here? I have to keep him with me."

"I'll keep him. Remember, I'm still on the payroll," Ramsey said.

Leicky and Biddings looked at each other questioningly.

"To help nab Kennard," I justified. "Give me a minute to get ready, and I'll meet you at the precinct."

I was getting a little too familiar with the East Precinct. When I arrived I found a parking space close to a ramp that lead to the fourth floor. When I reached the homicide squad, neither Leicky or Biddings were at there desks. One of the other detectives I saw on a previous visit nodded his head towards a room with a viewing glass.

Both detectives sat in the conference room with several other people. One of them, a tall, slender black man, stood over the others, motioning his hands wildly. From everyone's expression, I could tell that this was the ass chewing that Leicky had expected. I felt no obligation to enter the room, so I took a seat in the chair adjacent to Leicky's desk. After a few moments of counting the holes in the ceiling tiles, my eyes wandered on the desktop. And that's when I made my move.

I slipped the police file that Ramsey swiped underneath Leicky's desk calendar. No longer did I need to keep the file, revealing pictures of Shana's body sprawled in the Dumpster. The deep ache that gnawed at my soul was so unbearable that I was relieved to get rid of the file. Maybe the Bible was right; we are in a war between good and evil. I made a mental note to find that passage in the Bible, if I could, and read it. I wanted anwers – needed an explanation from a higher authority. This was definitely the work of inherent evil.

I snaked around a few desks, making my way to the conference room and entered. Looking at it from a Sears and Roebuck point of view, I assumed this was a manager's office, where he could look out on his working girls through the glass. A large table sat in the center of the room surrounded by six metal frame chairs padded with Herculon fabric. Comfort was definitely not a priority for the department's interior design.

The tall man that I saw bawling out Leicky and Biddings now sat at the head of the table. Across from them sat a clean-shaven white man wearing a dark blue suit, typical of an FBI agent with the exception of his head. When I took a closer look, however, the first thing that came to mind was Humpty Dumpty.

Next to Humpty was a black female, and from my angle, she looked to be rather short. She wore her dark brown hair in a bun and, like Humpty, she wore a dark blue suit.

Leicky gave the introductions. “This is Lt. Parker, homicide.”

I returned his nod.

“This is agent Kelly and Huffman from the FBI, Atlanta field office.”

Agent Kelly stood up to shake my hand. I was right, she was all of five two on the bathroom floor. I had thought the FBI had height and weight requirements to join the force, but again, that must have been another Hollywood myth.

Agent Huffman simply nodded.

Lt. Parker began. “We brought in Rick Edison to describe his investigation, albeit illegal, into the murder of his wife.” He turned from the FBI agents and looked at me. “Why don’t you walk us through, detail by detail.”

I looked at Leicky for support and when he gave a slight nod I began reciting the order of events after I found out about Shana’s murder. I don’t know what kind of truth serum had gotten into me, but I told them everything, including the AJC stunt that Kimi did with the Director Leggett at Emory. I felt somewhat proud when I saw the agent’s heads bend forward, concealing smirks.

“Did you see Dr. Van Hart after she stitched your wrist and before you met at Morton’s?” Agent Kelly asked, repeatedly going through her notes to get the names right.

“Like I said, I dropped off the 3-D image I got from Durden McDeevil.”

“So you entered the morgue on two separate occasions?” Huffman asked. When I nodded my head, he leaned over and whispered something in Kelly’s ear.

Out of the corner of my eye, I saw Leicky lean back, crossing his arms in disgust. The room remained silent for a moment, until Parker gestured me to continue. I explained how I found Kennard and the way he beat Scruffy at Grant Park.

“You paid seventy-five hundred dollars for a mutt to have surgery?” Kelly asked, with a look of compassion on her face.

“I felt sorry for him.”

Kelly gave Huffman a quick glance. When they turned their attention back to me, I told them about the telephone call and subsequent visit I got from Van Hart. I went on to explain the results from Lisa at the CDC and Van Hart’s updated results on the same matter.

“How did this Lisa from the CDC get a copy of the tox screen?” Agent Huffman asked and I had to decide how truthful I intended to be.

“I gave it to her.”

“Did Dr. Van Hart give you a copy?”

Everyone's head turned towards me. Something in me wanted to tell the truth, that Ramsey swiped it from Leicky's car, but I didn't want to incriminate him. So I went with the out they had given me. I didn't think Van Hart would object at this point. "Yes."

Huffman lowered his head. "Why would an accredited doctor give you, a nobody, vital information in the investigation of your wife? Tell me that."

"Because *nobody* else was investigating the case," I said, pissed off that he called me a nobody.

Agent Kelly whispered something in his ear. He thought about it and turned to me. "Is Lisa a doctor?"

"I'm not sure, but I think so."

"What's her last name?"

I looked surprised. "Why is that an issue?"

"Tell me her last name," he said rancorously. "You may have caused her death, too."

"Merriwether."

Huffman stood and walked to the corner of the room. He called someone from his cell phone and spoke inaudible words. A knot in my stomach tightened as I thought of Lisa's fate. Everyone in the room remained silent, almost holding their breath. It was strange to see Leicky and Biddings in the background of the questioning, not adding their two cents. But then again, the FBI was questioning me.

After Huffman ended the conversation, he sat back down. He nodded to Kelly.

"You seemed to like doctors, Mr. Edison. Did you and Van Hart have an affair?"

Up until that point, I came to peace with being open and honest, trying to assist the Atlanta Homicide and the FBI with the serial killer investigation, but he pulled the last straw. It just doesn't pay to be nice. "Agent Huffman, right?" I asked, cocky to the bone. "Never mind about my wife being a doctor. I suggest you worry about the article I'm going to submit to my colleague about how you let a serial killer roam the streets of Atlanta." I turned to Parker. "And Lieutenant, never mind about my investigation, albeit the only investigation, being illegal. I'll be sure to add the part that when I came to you for help, you arrested me. Think of the headlines, *Fire Hero Sought Help in Wife's Serial Murder*." I got up to leave. "You can sit here and accuse me of murdering my wife, having an affair with Van Hart," I looked at Leicky and Huffman. "You can accuse me of putting innocent women in harm's way, but you can't accuse me of sitting on my black ass taking this shit from the likes of all of you." I walked out the room, making sure to slam the door.

I hurried through the squad room to the ramp leading to the parking garage. I was finished dealing with these southern-fried idiots and their lagging investigation. I intended to start from scratch, beginning with the tapes. Before I reached the exit ramp door, I heard footsteps and Parker shouting something about checking the stairwell.

When I swung the door open, it stopped in mid-swing. I turned around and saw Agent Kelly with her foot wedged on the bottom of the door like a doorstop. She had some power for a little thing.

"Can I walk you to your car?" she simply asked. No groveling or pleading.

"Sure, why not."

When we walked side by side, I felt the depth of my size next to her.

"I'm sorry about all the testosterone flying in that room back there."

"What I don't understand is why am I the bad guy?"

"Mr. Edison, please try to understand the workings of an investigation. All shit rolls downhill and you are the lowest man on the totem pole."

"Call me Rick." Somehow she lost her FBI persona once we left the building and to my surprise, she was even personable. "Agent Kelly, I'm not even on the force, so why pick on me?"

"If it wasn't you, I guarantee it would've been me."

"But you had no involvement in–"

"It doesn't matter. The FBI is still a good-ole-boys club."

We made to the Expedition and I hesitated, not knowing what else to say. "Well, good luck on the investigation."

"Would it be possible for us to meet, one on one, for more questioning?" She turned and almost blocked me from opening the door. "It was so unfair to have you sit in the middle of that barrage."

"Sure, why not," I agreed, despite my earlier convictions.

18

We met at El Azteca Mexican restaurant in Midtown, taking in the city view from the patio. The sun made its descent and there wasn't a cloud in the sky. The night afforded us one of those exceptional mid-summer's gems where the humidity took a break from its relentless pounding. When the host saw Scruffy, he shrugged and got us seats closest to the street, where I tied him to the iron railing that separated us from the passing cars. We watched the colorful characters that made Midtown their home. What was once a neighborhood of Atlanta's elite, over the years the community became the haunt for the city's growing gay and lesbian populations.

Agent Kelly ordered the burrito supreme and I went for the chicken quesadillas. On my way to the restaurant, I had stopped at McDonald's and picked up two burgers for Scruffy. I had no intention of ever drinking tequila again, since it seemed that every time I did, someone died. But when I saw the pitcher of the smooth, frozen cocktail, I set my intentions aside. When she pulled out her notepad, I knew it was time for Q&A.

"I'd like to start from the very beginning. Do you know of anyone who would want to hurt your ex-wife?"

I turned my head and gazed at the young couple sitting across from us. I hadn't got a chance to get used to the term ex-wife. Two days after our divorce, she was murdered. When I heard the term now, I instinctively assumed people were talking about someone else.

I told her what I knew, seeing where her line of questioning was headed. She was trying to find some kind of connection with the two doctors, other than their ethnicities – and me.

"Do you know of anyone that would want to hurt you?"

"If someone wanted to hurt me, then why didn't they come after me instead of the women I knew?"

"Mr. Edison, criminal behavior is very complex, and though forensic pathologists like to think of it as an exact science, it isn't and probably never will be."

"That still doesn't answer my question. Why would someone kill Shana and Van Hart if it was me they wanted?"

She rubbed her chin as I had seen men do and I wondered if she was a lesbian. “Some profilists say that seeing their intended victim suffer over and over by the loss of loved ones is more satisfying than killing them.”

“What do you think?”

“I think, in this case, they may be right.”

When our food arrived, Agent Kelly had that look of hopeless frustration. It made me feel that she really cared to catch the killer. The evening ended with less fanfare than I had originally concluded and that was all right by me. Scruffy and me made our way back home before ten. He went to sleep, and so did I.

I started my shift at seven the next morning and felt the residual effects of two days of tequila, without a pounding at my door with news of another murder. The guys gave my looks ranging from disdain to disbelief when I bought Scruffy in. Cap went as far to say that the department only accepted Dalmatians as the mascot. I kindly told him where to shove it.

True to her reputation, Naia stood by the stove whipping up breakfast. And true to form, the guys sat at the table for their share-and-stare. As I joined the crew and sat around the kitchen table, I still couldn’t nix the feeling of knowing her.

Later that day, Ramsey and I saw her and JT in a quite conversation and we smiled about JT being the first to sleep with her. Our conversation was interrupted by the alarm. It was the first since Briarcliff Summit and I felt a smidgen of unease rush through me.

We arrived at a community of older Victorian houses in Candler Park. When we turned down a narrow street, I saw no smoke, no flames and no crowds of nosy people. What I did see, however, was a middle-aged woman rushing to the rig in her robe and yelling something nobody could hear. Her hair was pulled up and wrapped in a silk scarf.

With the siren off, we looked down at her, curious.

“My house is possessed by the devil,” she screamed. “Get him out.”

Cap gave her a contemptuous look and nodded in our direction. “OK, ma’am, just show us where the devil is.”

“I’ll show you all right, he’s right in my den.”

She led the way from the street, up her walkway, into her house and into the small paneled den. The room smelled like a mothball manufacturing plant, with a hint of buttered toast.

We positioned ourselves near the back wall where she pointed, and listened for the devil. Cap raised a hand and we stood in silence for a few seconds. Fulton County Fire Department policy was to answer all calls, no matter how outrageous. The trainer informed us, years back when we were rookies, that a smoldering fire could sound like fiery spirits from hell.

Then we heard it. At first it sounded like scratching and then, after the entire crew stepped in closer, we heard something softer, more desperate. It was the life call of some kittens that were caught between the house frame and the drywall. Moving into action, Ramsey went for the ax and I went for the search cam, a mini-laproscopy for viewing tight areas. Cap explained to the woman that we would have to gain access to the tiny area. With her permission, Ramsey swung the ax, making a small hole in the wall.

After a few moments of calibrating the search cam, I was able to locate the kittens, eight in all. They were the tiniest critters I had ever seen. When I gave Ramsey the coordinates, he gently made another hole in the drywall, nearer to the kittens. We plucked them out one by one, satisfied with our success.

Naia found an old laundry basket that the lady said we could have, and placed them inside. I saw a gentler side of her which touched my heart in places that had been vacant for a long time. After we finished cleaning up the mess to the best of our ability, we left the house and to our surprise, a Fox 5 News reporter was camped by the rig with her cameraman. It surprised me how quickly the media was able to dispatch their field crews to our location moments after we arrived, even though it really shouldn't have.

Not wanting to be the brunt of the department's jokes I dashed out of view and let them have at the kitten-carrying Naia. Ramsey and I watched the Fox 5 reporter pounce on her. We smiled at each other as she pleaded in the camera for adoptive parents.

Little did she know that the entire local 410 would dub her the Kitten Lady.

When we made it back to the 23rd, I saw the Battalion Chief's truck parked next to a Crown Victorian. Cap jumped out of the rig as we backed it in and checked the equipment, a mandatory duty after each call out. While I replaced the search cam in its proper place, Cap came out and stood next to me.

"BC needs you in the kitchen."

"What does he want with me?"

"Why don't you to go find out for yourself." He placed his hands in his pocket and tried to look casual. "Here, let me take that."

He took the search cam from me and all but pushed me on into the kitchen. I got nervous when I saw the Battalion Chief sitting across from Huffman, old egghead.

"Why don't you sit down, Edison," Battalion Chief Sheldon said.

"What's the problem?"

Huffman eyed me carefully. "Agent Kelly is in the hospital."

"What? What happened to her?" I asked, horrified of what I thought he was going to say next. "I was just with her last night–"

"It seems she was run off the road last night. We need you to come to the field office."

"Is she dead?"

"She made it, but we need you to come with us now."

"I can't leave in the middle of my shift–"

"Never mind about that," Sheldon interrupted. "As of now, you are on personal leave, with pay."

"Leave? I don't understand."

"We're putting you in protective custody until we find the person responsible for this," Huffman said blankly.

I started getting defensive, but told myself to stay cool. "What does Kelly getting into an accident have to do with putting me in protective custody?"

"She wasn't in an accident. She was run off the road." Huffman gave me a contemptuous look. "You were with Dr. Van Hart the day she was murdered. You were with Agent Kelly the night someone attempted murder on her." He paused. "Getting the picture now?"

I looked at Sheldon for some kind of rationale, but he glanced down. "Are you saying that all these murders and attempted murders are because of me?"

"You got it," Huffman answered. "Every time you are with a woman, she somehow gets herself killed."

I wiped my hands on my trousers, thinking fast. "But I wasn't with my wife the day she got killed."

"Edison, just go with Agent Huffman and get this thing resolved. Don't worry about your job, it'll be here when you get back." Sheldon stood up. "And that's an order."

19

The FBI field office was located in the Richard B. Russell building on Mitchell Street, downtown. I still had on my uniform as I followed Huffman to the fourteenth floor. Even though the city had banned smoking in government buildings nine years ago, the building still smelled of stale cigarette smoke. When we made it up to the office, I was disappointed. I had expected to see elaborate computer systems and wall monitors surrounding the floor with sophisticated agents pacing back and forth, like a movie scene. But all I got was an open floor plan with those cubicle-styled offices. On the perimeter of the floor were smaller, private offices with expensive wooden doors. Huffman led me to one of those private offices, and when the door closed behind us, it felt like a vacuum chamber.

I took a seat across from the desk while Huffman rummaged through his files. I noticed a small television set bolted to the corner wall and wondered why the FBI field agents found it necessary to have a television in their offices.

"Is Agent Kelly going to be all right?" I asked, trying to break the thick silence.

"She'll make it," Huffman said, not looking up from his files.

"Can you explain why you're putting me in protective custody?"

He stopped, giving me a thoughtful glare. "It's not the protective custody you are thinking about." He went back to his search. "I'm going to bring you up to speed on the plan."

"What plan?" I asked, feeling helpless.

"It seems someone doesn't want you in the company of women and we want to plant a decoy with you to bring out the killer. Elementary stuff."

I blinked hard, trying to understand what he just said. "Where did you get that theory?"

He stopped again, this time finding the file he was looking for. He opened it and placed three photos on the desk. One of Shana, Van Hart and Agent Kelly. "Simple, you were married to her." He pointed to Shana's picture, the one she took for the American Medical Association. "You were at Morton's Steakhouse with Dr. Van Hart." He slid the picture of her closer to me. "And you were at a Mexican restaurant having margaritas with Agent Kelly."

I considered his logic. "That makes sense, if this was Crime Solving 101. But, besides me, you don't have any other connection. Still pretty weak, don't you think?"

He looked at me smugly. "Better than your Kennard connection. What made you think that he was capable of knowing Emory's security?"

"At least I had something. Atlanta PD had zilch."

"You are the connection, Mr. Edison. Agent Kelly has been with the bureau nearly seventeen years without so much as a scratch, and the day she has dinner with you, someone tries to kill her."

"That may have been an isolated incident, just a drunk driver."

"Before the doctor sedated her, she informed us it was deliberate." Huffman said, like we were in some kind of word match. He was getting angry. "Can you think of any reason someone may want to kill the women in your life?"

"No, just like I told Agent Kelly."

"Well, sit tight and we'll go over the plan. I'll introduce you to your new female companion. We'll plant you two in open places and watch both of you."

"Someone from the FBI will be watching my every move?"

"Yes."

"What about my job?"

"We'll be watching there too." He stood up to leave. "Maybe we'll have your new girlfriend bring you dinner."

Huffman smirked at his lame joke and opened the door. "I'll be right back. I'm going to find you a woman."

Now I knew what Kelly meant about the good-ole-boys-club. I waited in the office for nearly ten minutes, staring at the walls. I felt awkward and antsy, so I decided to turn on the small television set bolted to the wall. I switched it to the News at Noon on Fox 5. The first thing I saw was pre-recorded scene of the 23rd exiting the house with the demon cats. When I saw Naia coming into frame with the basket of kittens, I smiled to myself, thankful that I wasn't the one in the limelight. As she pleaded for adoptive parents, I cocked my head, again thinking how familiar she looked and deciding I would ask her first chance. Then Huffman walked in with a woman.

He made the introductions. "It's all set up. Just go back to work and I'll send Agent Boggs to the station with a basket of food." He let out another smirk. "Hope you like Italian?"

When I returned to the station, Scruffy jumped on my legs. His seemingly overnight recovery boggled my mind. The other guys surrounded the television and I made my way back to the bunkroom. Scruffy followed me as I patted his head, remembering the awful beating he withstood. I walked through the engine room and that's when I saw it.

I caught a glimpse of Naia from the chrome plate on the rig. From my distorted view, she hoisted herself up from a horizontal bar near the gear room. It was amazing to see such strength from a woman, because not only did she perform the underhanded grip, she also wore a twenty-pound barbell plate attached to a belt harness. While I stood there looking into the chrome, she'd done ten reps from a full hang position, effortlessly. Then something caught my eye. I leaned closer to the rig and saw it. The fear that gnawed at my heart was so gripping that my throat constricted. She had a three-inch scar on her right wrist. The wound had healed and formed a keloid scar similar to the Omega sign carved on the arms of Omega Psi Phi Fraternity brothers. I remembered Leicky mentioning something about the killer having *one helluva scar*. When I tried to back away, I hit my head on one of the compartment doors, making a noticeable thump noise. When I cut my eyes back to Naia, her gaze bore down on me and in that instant, I feared for my life. Those menacing eyes pierced through me.

Instinctively I reached in the compartment and pulled out the search cam. I immediately went to the kitchen and started toiling with it. I was so nervous that my hands started shaking so violently that I had to grab one in order to steady both of them. Twenty minutes later, Naia came in and started cooking dinner. I didn't know what to say. Had she really seen me through the chrome? If she did and I remained silent, then she'd know that I knew. If she wasn't able to make me out and I remained silent, then I could call the FBI and tell them who the killer was. But either way, I needed to protect myself.

"I saw you up there," I said and pointed to the engine room. "You're pretty tight."

She smiled. "Why thank you," she said, pausing slightly. "Took years to get to that level."

"I would imagine it did, indeed."

Scruffy stood by the door, vying for attention. This time I could not indulge him. I had to do something, and quickly. I paced around the rest of my shift in a daze. Ramsey asked several times if I was sick. After the second time, I played on that plot and began holding my stomach as if I was suffering from some kind of bug. That served two purposes; one – to let on that I was feeling ill, and two – to dismiss myself from eating Naia's cooking.

While the other guys ate, I sat in the day room and tried to collect my thoughts. That's when Naia came in and crouched down next to me. I felt a cold shiver race through my body, making the hairs on my neck stand up. I wanted to scream, *somebody help me*, but I was too afraid to move. I felt her evil presence next to me.

"I could make you some homemade chicken soup for your stomach," she offered.

"Um – I'm afraid it will come back up if I eat it. But thanks anyway." She stood to leave and I felt a wave of relief wash over me. I had to make a decision whether to call Huffman from the FBI or tell Leicky about my discovery. But first, I needed to know if what I thought was true.

Just when I focused on my dilemma, I heard a knock on the dayroom door. I got off the couch and answered, thinking it was someone wanting a blood pressure check.

When I opened the door, I saw Agent Boggs and remembered the FBI decoy. She wore casual clothes and carried a picnic basket. I had to get her out of there, because if I was right, she'd be the next victim.

"Hi, can we do this another time, something just came up?" I whispered, pushing her out the door.

"Sorry, I have to follow the plan," she said as she hugged me and maneuvered herself back in the doorway. "By the way, first name is Theresa," she whispered.

From the corner of my eye, I saw Smelly lean over his chair and smile. Then Naia walked in and looked at us with a curious expression. I shifted my weight from one foot to the other, not knowing what to do. Theresa, in her innocence of the situation, stood there like a woman protecting the sanctity of her relationship.

"Naia, this is a good friend of mine, Theresa."

They exchanged hellos and Naia went back in the kitchen. I grabbed the basket and nudged Theresa out the door. The sun cast a purplish haze on the horizon and even though it was going down, it still felt like one hundred degrees outside.

"We're going to eat in the car," I said boldly.

"That's a good idea. That way, if someone is eyeing you, they'll see us."

If she only knew.

We sat in the car and I looked at the food like it was some kind of parasite. I was actually hungry, but the knot in my stomach wouldn't cooperate. I had to think of a plan and fast. I looked at Theresa and thought about telling her, but something stopped me. I wanted Leicky and Biddings to get the credit since they had to retrace their steps to get another police file.

When Theresa was satisfied with the first phase of the FBI's plan, she left the parking lot and left me alone with Naia. I went back in and sat next to Ramsey, who was talking to Tamara on the phone. I felt safe sitting next to him. Then, I had a thought. I took a deep breath and began my plan of action.

Naia was in the kitchen cleaning up the dinner dishes. I walked up to her.

"Why don't you let me finish up here," I said, trying to act normal. "My stomach is feeling a little better, why don't you make us some coffee?"

"That sounds like a plan." She seemed to beam at the idea.

I finished up the dishes while she brewed a fresh pot of coffee. I set out the cups, sugar and cream, being careful to get two different color cups. We sat down at the table for a contrived chat.

"So Naia, what brings you to the department?" I asked, trying to sound interested.

"Oh, several reasons, but the main one is that this career is basically recession proof."

"Most women don't think like that."

"Most women haven't seen what I've seen."

The way she said that last statement made me wonder. What had she seen?

We continued to drink coffee and when I was satisfied I had gotten what I wanted, I cleared the table and told her I'd clean up the mess. She seemed agreeable and mentioned that she needed to finish her workout routine. When she cleared the kitchen, I acted quickly.

20

After a long night of nervous sleep, I woke the next morning and rushed home. I called Ramsey on my way.

"I have some news about the killer."

"The FBI find your guy?" he asked.

"No, and I can't tell you over the phone." I turned on the interstate and hit the gas hard. "Come by the office as soon as you can and I'll explain."

I heard hesitation in his voice. "Today's the big day, man. I'm proposing to Tamara."

"Ramsey, I need you today more than ever." I got in the HOV lane, hoping the police weren't around. "Can't you wait till tomorrow?"

"Rick, I'm sorry, but the restaurant is all set up."

I sighed in disgust. "All right, man, bye." I hung up and felt bad for being so short with him.

I made it home in record time, took a shower and left for the office. The coffee cup I swiped from Naia was in a plastic bag and I decided to give it to Leicky instead of the FBI. Maybe it was the guilt I felt, but I was comfortable with my decision. If he could match the DNA from her saliva to the blood from the Dumpster, I could prove my case. I called Leicky and left an urgent message when he didn't answer.

While stuck in traffic on my way to the office, I brooded over Naia's motive. It made no sense. Was she just a crazed serial killer, choosing random victims that, by coincidence, I knew? Or was there an inherently evil method to her madness? I tried Leicky again, still no answer.

When I finally made it to the building, I didn't bother speaking to Doc Jones. Scruffy and me raced up the stairs and I tried Leicky. Then I called Biddings and he wasn't at his desk, either.

I waited ten more minutes before I called again, still to no avail. Scruffy had been looking hungry, so I checked my watch – too early for Mandarin Gardens Chinese restaurant to be open, so I took him for a walk downtown to find some food. My stomach was empty as well.

I walked up Marietta Street and turned on Mitchell. The smog hovered around the city's skyscrapers, blocking the sun's torment on my skin. We walked until we found a small restaurant boasting a soul food sign. The place was called Norma-Lee and when I asked the heavyset woman who took my order what the name meant, she said her name was Norma and her husband's name was Lee. "Norma-Lee, normally, get it?" she asked.

When we made it back to the office, I decided to kill some time and speak with Doc, but he wasn't in. His door was unlocked, though but I shrugged it off and made my way upstairs. I began eating and gave Scruffy his breakfast and decided to call the precinct one more time. Still the same verdict, both detectives were out.

After wolfing down my food, I felt restless and irritable. I thought about calling Agent Huffman with my new lead, but quickly nixed the idea. I was going stir crazy and for no particular reason, I wanted a cigarette. Then I gave in to my craving and ran across the street to the pharmacy and bought a pack of Kool Mild cigarettes. I lit the first cigarette on my way back and enjoyed it.

I missed having Van Hart around to bounce ideas back and forth. I felt a pang of guilt for missing her only when I needed a favor. I thought about calling Kimi, but I quickly dismissed that idea in fear that she may be Naia's next victim. Then something hit me. Why was Kimi overlooked? Did Naia only kill African-American doctors? I had more questions than answers. *Damn, I wish Ramsey or somebody was here.*

My thoughts went to how confident I was in thinking that Kennard was Shana's killer and that was an error of judgment on my part. Now here I sat thinking Naia was the killer just because she had a scar on her wrist. I looked to the ceiling and said a silent prayer thanking God that I wasn't a detective, for real.

After some time had passed, I decided to call the desk sergeant and leave a message with him. I had to think hard to remember his name. Andrews? Andretti? Amos. That was it – Sergeant Amos.

"Sergeant Amos, this is Rick Edison, and I don't know if you remember me or not but I was there when you–"

"I remember you, all right. What can I do for you?"

"I am desperately trying to reach Detective Leicky or Biddings. I have some vital information on my wife's case."

"Must be a full moon, everybody's busy around here. They went out on a call early this morning."

"Can I go to where they are?"

"Not allowed. They are processing a crime scene."

"All right, then get a pen."

I explained to Amos the urgency of the information I received, and in a vague way, I told him that I didn't want to give it to the FBI, but that I would if I didn't hear back from them. He took all my information including my location. After we hung up, I felt better having spoken to someone.

I wanted to call Dana, but feared she'd hear the nervousness in my voice. In the meantime, I decided to view the tapes of Emory one more time. Now that I had a face to look for, I stood a better chance of collecting the right evidence.

My eyelids became heavy as I sat and watched the doldrums of the scenes I had seen so many times. But it seemed like another time and place. I hadn't noticed before, but the machine even had a voice recorder. That didn't make any sense to include a recorder with such an elaborate device. But who am I to judge? The phone rang and jolted me out of my daze. I picked it up before it finished its first ring cycle.

"Hello."

All I heard was a dial tone and I quickly called *69 to find out if it was Leicky. The recorded voice said that the service could not reach or callback that number. I began biting my knuckles, wondering if it was Leicky calling from a cell phone. I lit another cigarette and somehow it was less satisfying than the first one.

I settled back down and stared at the tapes. Scruffy lay on the floor, not wanting for anything. Soon, it became more difficult for me to keep my eyes open. In an attempt to keep busy, I dialed Leicky's desk one more time. After another failed attempt, I lay back in the swivel chair and watched and waited.

A rustling noise jolted me out of a deep sleep. I had no idea that I was that tired. When I opened my eyes the sun was on its way down. When I rubbed the sleep from my eyes, Scruffy barked and stared at the door. Then I heard the noise again. I smiled, thinking about the crack addict who attempted to break in my office two months ago. I decided to play with him this time.

I went to the door, not worrying about being seen through the privacy glass, and opened it.

Naia stood there calmly, almost too cool. She wore a black, one-piece suit that clung to her curves. Fear hadn't reached my brain yet, but as soon as she raised the gun that she concealed behind her back, I felt it. I faced death square on for the first time in my life. Instantly I thought of Dana and how I would miss her sweet sixteen party, her first broken heart and her senior prom.

Naia pulled the trigger.

21

The bullet entered my right shoulder and my body instantly felt rigid. My legs gave in and I crumbled to the floor like someone plucked all the bones from my body. Then Scruffy jumped up and clamped his teeth around her wrist like he was a trained attack dog. With her free hand, Naia pointed the gun at him and shot him in the chest. He fell to the ground, listless. I looked over at Scruffy and my heart sank at his misfortune in life.

I was slowly dying. I never knew what a bullet wound felt like, but somehow, I thought the pain would have been worse. I felt a sensation in the area where she shot me, but not excruciating pain. I always thought of dying as floating toward some kind of bright light, but my mental faculties remained intact and I didn't see any light.

"Just lie there like a good boy," Naia said as she stepped into the office, closing the door behind her.

She grabbed a backpack that had been slung around her shoulder, and while she searched for something, she bent down and embedded her knee in my recently recovered shoulder, rendering me useless. I tried to get up, but my body didn't respond to the command.

"There's no need to move. You won't be able to use your command and control functions of your body."

I was gripped with fear as I tried to ask her what she meant, but the words failed to escape my mouth. Why was my body failing me? I tried to move again, but it was useless.

She pulled out a roll of duct tape and taped my ankles together. Next, she placed a piece of tape around my mouth. It was hard for me to breathe and for a moment, I thought I would suffocate on my own bile. The pain in my shoulder was dulling and I wondered how long I had to live.

"Come on, my love, let's get you up."

I was amazed at her strength as she pulled me up to the desk chair. It would take a man a grunt or two what she accomplished effortlessly. I looked at her with panicked eyes and she let out an evil Cruella DeVille laugh from *101 Dalmatians*, and I almost expected her to say, *I want those puppies.*

She tied my hands behind my back and I felt something prick my wrist.

I felt something.

I made a mental command to move my finger and it worked. My control functions were coming back. As if reading my mind, Naia reached for the gun and shot me in the thigh. A ripple of pain streamed through my body and I was unable to move.

I got a closer look the gun and saw that is wasn't a pistol. It looked like some kind of specialty gun but this one, instead of a bullet, it shot out two pellets that neither pierced my flesh nor hurt it. It just sent a pulse of energy into my thigh.

"Now it's time for some goodies." She reached in the sack and pulled out a clear glass vial with white pills inside. "If I keep on poking you with this Taser gun, you'll be paralyzed."

Since she didn't want to paralyze me, I feared some kind of torture.

She took two pills out, yanked the tape from my mouth and stuffed them in.

"I want you to experience the same feeling that your wife had."

My eyes looked around wildly as I recalled Van Hart saying that Shana had high levels of Oxycontin in her system. Knowing that I was about to experience the same fate as Shana made me wish I were already dead.

She quickly tore off fresh tape and placed it over my mouth. I tried not to swallow the pills but the acid in my mouth quickly dissolved them into gritty, sand-like granules. I felt scared being alone with this psychopath. The fear of the unknown was worse than dying.

Naia got up and stood by the window. "Did you think I was going to fall for that coffee cup stunt you pulled?" She stretched her arms as if she were about to settle down and read a Danielle Steel novel. "I guess you learned a few tricks on forensics from your doctor friend. I wish I could've been there when they discovered her body in the morgue."

I tried to turn my head to look at her but it wouldn't move. *Damn!* My mind raced, trying to think why she targeted me. I could not place her anywhere in my life.

"Oh, I forgot, you probably don't remember me since I lost fifty or so pounds." She rolled me from behind the desk to in front of the couch where she took a seat. "Actually, my trainer tells me I lost more than fifty because most of that fat turned into hard-core muscle."

I blinked in amazement. That's who she reminded me of – Natasha. I met her at a party about three years ago. It was a pool party that one of my buddies from college had given. Shana went with me and complained about leaving Dana. I knew she didn't particularly care for the rowdy crowd so I told her I would hitch a ride with one of the fellows. I stayed on and got full-tilt drunk. I saw Naia sitting on a lawn chair by herself and felt sorry that no one paid her any attention. She had a cute face but she was a big girl. I went over and began conversing and to my chagrin, she was wonderful company with a beautiful personality.

She took me home that night and for no reason, I kissed her. After that, I called her frequently, enjoying lively conversations. I went to her apartment on Glenwood Road and was delighted by her elaborate meals. She treated me like a king and I thoroughly enjoyed myself in her company. Not only could I relax and be myself, but I didn't have to spend a bunch of money trying to bedazzle her. But when I finally made love to her, she became a possessive maniac. She called me ten times a day, professing her love and begging me to visit her again. She threatened to kill herself if she couldn't have me. It was too much strain. Gone were the easy conversations and warm atmosphere, and I had to end the affair, changing my cell phone number and dropping off the face of her earth.

And now here she was, back in my life again. I heard a crackling noise and looked at Scruffy. He remained still and I feared the worst. Naia retrieved a cell phone from her backpack.

"Yeah," Naia spoke into the two-way.

"Wolf here, the stork has arrived."

"Good. Papa bear in the hole." She turned to me. "Everything's going on as planned, sweetie."

I didn't think that I was able to feel more horror than I was already experiencing, but knowing that she was working with someone else made my bile rise.

"So you remember me now, Rick-E." She let out a smile and I confirmed that it was her. "I just love the nickname the guys at the 23rd gave you."

My eyes lit up as I thought about the fire department. How did she get on with the department? It was coming back to me. She was a caseworker at the welfare department.

Then everything began to get fuzzy. My head felt like it was spinning. I tried to blink the dizziness away, but any movement made me nauseous. Then I heard the door open and looked up to see a man carrying something in a blanket. I strained to focus, but my vision blurred. When he stepped closer, I saw that it was JT. He wore a black wig over his bald head and I realized that he was the man from the surveillance tapes. I wanted to scream out in agony. No pain that I experienced could compare to the panic that overtook me when JT removed the blanket. It was Dana.

He placed her lifeless body on the couch. I struggled to get out of the chair, but it was useless. I felt hopeless. I strained to see if her chest was moving – I had to know if she was still alive. When I saw her little chest raise, I lowered my head and wept in relief.

JT stood next to me and yanked the tape off my mouth. I squirmed to get away from him and when I did, I felt that pinch on my wrist. I recalled how I splintered the chair rail a few weeks earlier. On instinct, I began sawing through the tape with the sharp fragment.

"She won't be living too long," JT said in a hair-raising tone.

I withered violently to escape the confines of the chair. I wanted to dig my fist in his heart and yank it out. He grabbed me by the back of head and both JT and Naia towered over me

"She will die the same way your wife did. And you will see and suffer through it."

"Why?" I asked, the words coming out in a whisper. I cut my eyes and saw Naia smiling.

"Why, my friend, is because you need to suffer the pain and agony just like we did," JT said. He pulled off the black wig.

What was he talking about? How did JT suffer like Naia? Naia turned my head toward her.

"When you stopped calling me," Naia said, "my life had ended, Rick. You see, you were the center of my life." She kissed me. "We shared intimacy."

I tried to jerk away from her advance, all the while working the tape off. "Can you say it, Rick, in-to-me-you-see. Intimacy is what we shared." She kissed me again.

"When my wife left me, it was you who sewed the last stitch in our divorce," JT said.

"What are you talking about? I never even met your wife." I pleaded.

"Valerie, Rick. You remember now?"

I did remember her. She approached me at one of the grocery stores where I worked security. "JT, she came on to me. I didn't know she was your wife. You got to believe me."

"You need to be taught a lesson about sticking your cock in another man's foxhole."

I looked at Naia, then at JT, unsure of the connection between them both. "Why, how did you two get together?"

It was Naia who spoke. "When I found you at the 23rd, it was JT who answered the phone. The stars aligned perfectly." She rubbed my thighs and worked her way to my inner thighs. The thought of her touching me made my skin crawl. Then I saw a shadow through the privacy glass. Ramsey opened the door and walked in.

"What's going on in here?" he asked.

"Run, Ramsey!" I yelled.

With the swiftness of a trained killer, JT reached around his backside and pulled out a Glock 9 mm. He aimed at Ramsey's chest and pulled the trigger.

"Nooooo." I hollered after I heard the thunderous blast from the gun.

Ramsey staggered two steps back and grabbed his chest. A bewildered gaze came over him as he back up to the wall and sank to the floor. The tape began loosening.

JT turned back to me. "Let's start with pretty little Dana over there." He nodded toward my daughter. "Shall I begin with the eyes?"

I flinched, thinking about Shana's eyes. Every time I was afforded a movement, I worked at the tape.

"Do it slow," Naia said and pulled out an ice pick from the backpack.

Then the telephone rang. Naia immediately jumped up and grabbed a knife from her backpack. She moved to the wall and sliced the cord coming from the jack.

I had to stall them. I needed to think of a way to get them talking.

"How did you manage to get back in my life?" I asked.

She smiled with an evil slant. "That is the beauty, Rick-E. You see, when I made contact with JT, I devised a plan. I lost the weight in order to pass the CPAT–"

"Why did you want to take the Candidate Physical Aptitude Test?" I interrupted her while working the tape.

"Don't mistake me, Rick-E." Naia dragged out the *E* in Rick-E that made my flesh crawl. "Never interrupt me again, or I'll make this worse on you than you can ever imagine."

I nodded my head in submission.

"I took the CPAT so we could see you suffer after I eliminated your wife."

The knot that built up in my stomach felt like a bomb had exploded when I heard the word *eliminate* leave her mouth. My infidelity caused the death of my wife. At that moment, I felt a bitter detachment from life. I no longer cared what happened to me. In fact, I wished for the jaws of death to crush me right here right now. Then I looked over to Dana.

Naia stopped and gazed at JT with a look of disgust on her face. "But JT couldn't get me transferred in time."

"I told you, I had no control over that."

"Shut up. It's too late for that now." She raised her hands in disgust.

I heard dissention between them and I had to find a way to make it work for me. "How did you get to the 23rd?"

"You remember that little fire at the Briarcliff Summit?"

"No one was supposed to die, Naia. I told you I just wanted one of them hurt – not killed," JT scorned.

"Would you stop your babbling, you spineless piece of shit."

I noticed that JT drew back. Then out of my peripheral vision, I saw Ramsey stir. I had to keep their attention on me.

"Naia, you want to know the reason I stopped calling you?" I asked, reaching for anything.

She stopped and looked at me. "Humor me."

"Our relationship was going so good until we made love." I paused, giving Ramsey time to come to. "I didn't mind the blubber around your fat ass, but after I smelled your foul pussy, I couldn't take it anymore. I just hope that you lost that rank smell when you lost some of that weight."

I got what I wanted after I saw the look of total shock come over her. She was rendered speechless. Ramsey's eyes were open and I went after JT.

"And JT, I didn't know Valerie was your wife. In fact I thought she had been single for a long time judging by the number of orgasms I gave her. Bam Bam Bam, back to back." I paused again. "You ever made sweet Val cum that many times?"

It came so quickly that I didn't have time to duck. He punched me in the jaw so hard I thought I heard bones cracking. But I had to remain focused. When he hit me, the force gave me just enough movement to break my hands free from the tape. My hands were free but I had to play it cool. JT lifted another hand and I was prepared for it, but it never came.

"Stop. Can't you see what he's trying to do?" She looked at him and that gave me a escape to check on Ramsey. He nodded his head that he was ready. I gave him three blinks – one, two and three.

Ramsey got up and charged JT, knocking him down. I threw both my fists around and made contact with Naia's temples. She stumbled but regained her composure. She swung the ice pick. When I tried to move my leg, I tripped, because my legs were still taped together. She made a movement with the ice pick and I turned on my side and swiped her legs from underneath her. The woman moved like a cougar, pouncing on me. She struck me in my damaged shoulder with the ice pick and I felt a searing pain rip through me. Then I heard a gunshot ring out. Naia and I looked up to see Ramsey and JT lying on the floor. Blood oozed out and the look on Ramsey's face said it all. My strength was leaving fast and I tried one last attempt at the temples. She blocked it and came down again with the ice pick. With Ramsey dead, and me losing strength, I knew that I didn't have a chance in hell to come out of this alive. Then I heard it.

"Freeze. Drop your weapon," Leicky's voice bellowed.

The relief that I felt was unmasked by any other. But it was shortlived. Naia wrapped her arms around my neck and lifted me up while sticking the ice pick near my neck.

"Back up or I'll rip his throat out."

I saw Dana on the couch and I had a reason to live. I mustered all the strength I could find and elbowed her in the rib cage. I felt the pressure of the knife release and I dropped to the floor. The loud explosion of bullets rang in my ear and I turned to see Naia grabbing her chest and looking shocked that she had been shot. Her body backed up. then she looked at the ice pick and made a motion of momentum to swing it, Leicky and Biddings opened fire on her and her body jerked, recoiling as each bullet ripped through her flesh.

In one smooth motion, the force of the bullets propelled Naia's body back against the large window on the other side of the room. One of the bullets hit the glass and her body, in its perpetual motion shattered the glass and fell out of the window.

Leicky and Biddings ran to the window and turned their heads in disgust.

I crawled over to Dana and lay my head gently on her chest. "Wake up, baby, please wake up for Daddy." I kissed her face and the tears left my eyes. "Please wake up."

Her eyes blinked open and I cried more. "You came back, Dana, you came back."

She looked at me strangely. "Daddy, your breath stinks."

I laughed so hard that the pain in my shoulder reminded me that I needed medical attention. I removed the tape from my ankles and got up. I saw Ramsey sitting up with the gun still in his hands.

"I came by to tell you Tamara said yes."

I heard a yelp and looked at Scruffy. His body had regained its motor control and he was squirming. I looked over at Leicky, who spoke into his cell phone, and gave him a warm smile. When I reached the window and peered down, I saw the moon cast its glow in the pool of blood from Naia's body. She lay there next to the eerie scarlet moon.

22

They kept me in the hospital for three days and I was thankful because it gave me time to reflect on the sins of my past. My infidelity caused so much pain and anguish that I felt a bitter detachment. My spirits immediately lifted when I saw Dana bounce in with Aisha.

"Daddy, I got out of the hospital before you." She jumped on my bed and this time it was OK. "The doctors and nurses said I can eat all the ice cream I want. Didn't they, Auntie Aisha?"

"Yes, they did."

I felt so relieved that she was safe. Those bastards fed her Oxycontin to sedate her. The doctor informed me that had it been a higher dose, she would have died. When Aisha tried to explain how they grabbed her, I held up my hand – I just wanted to sit there and enjoy my daughter. She told me Ramsey's surgery went well and that he was expected to recover one hundred percent.

"Dana, baby, what do you say I buy a big house on the same street as your Aunt Aisha?"

"Oh daddy, can we? Then I could spend the night anytime I want."

"Spend the night with me?" I asked, feeling hurt that she thought of me as a spend-the-night-father.

"No silly. I mean I could spend the night with Auntie Aisha." She bit her lower lip. "But do we have to keep that ugly dog?"

"He's part of our family."

I smiled at her and gave her a hug when Kimisha walked in. She was so beautiful and she gave me a look like my grandmother used to after I hurt myself.

"Aisha, can you take Dana down to the car? I'll be right there."

Kimi sat on the bed and gave me a once over. "You did it, just like you said."

"Yeah, I guess I did." I gazed out of the window, thinking about the ordeal that plagued my life.

Kimi looked at me in an enticing way. "Would you like to go out sometime?"

I thought about it. She was smart and beautiful, the kind of woman you could take home. But I had to learn to love me and not depend on women to satisfy the empty hole that lived in my soul. “Kimi, can we just be friends?”

*

Printed in the United States
1270200003B/28

9 781413 700732